THE GHOSTS OF
WINTHROP MANOR

A NOVEL BY
LINDY MICHAELS

This book is a work of fiction. All names, characters, places and descriptions are a product of the author's imagination. Any resemblance to actual persons, living or dead is entirely coincidental.

Cover Design Artwork by
Tiffany Miller/ TifanyMillerMosaics.com
'Ghosted Up' by Deborah Gordon

<u>DEDICATED TO:</u>

To my amazing daughters, Erin and Shani and, of course, my fantastic grandchildren, Ethan, Mia, Cierra and Zoë Rose.

To couples everywhere, whom I hope this book, through laughter and truths, helps you to live happily ever after in the here and now.

A special thanks to my wonderful friend, Deborah Gordon, who 'ghosted up' Tiffany Miller's mosaic of 'The Dancers.'

A special thanks to Karin Buchak for doing all the techno book stuff I would have had no idea how to do!

CHAPTER ONE

RANDOLPH WINTHROP THE FIRST AND MILDRED

The great Winthrop Manor had seen better days. Much better days. Built at the turn of the twentieth century, overlooking the Hollywood Hills, it was a beacon of ostentatious glamour. Randolph Winthrop The First had built the castle for his princess, his love, the shy, unassuming and beautiful Mildred, his wife-to-be.

He had inherited his vast fortune from his grandfather, Rudolph Winthrop The Fifth. Rudolph was a horse thief, in a long line of horse thieves and did quite well for himself. When his only son, Rudolph The Sixth decided not to follow in his father's footsteps, or hooves, as the son liked to joke, and become an artiste, actually a juggler, of little renown, it must be added, Rudolph The Fifth put down his... foot. "Never again will there be a Rudolph the Seventh, Eighth, Ninth or any Rudolph Winthrop, ever, again! You have shamed this family! You have shamed our great name!"

But when a wee boy was born to his outcast son by a barmaid floozy and when said son was shot and killed in a drunken barroom fight, soon after, Rudolph Winthrop The Fifth stole the babe, while the barmaid continued to flooze, raised him as his own and renamed him Randolph. "Willie?! Willie?! No Winthrop, while I'm alive, will be saddled with the name Willie!" he was overheard screaming. And thus did come to pass a new dynasty in the City Of Angels, that of the Randolph Winthrop's.

Randolph Winthrop The First also did quite well for himself, under the harsh tutelage of his grandfather, dabbling in horse-thieving, dog racing, and gambling, but that was nothing compared to the mounds of money left to him by his grand-pappy when he died. "Do me proud," the old man hoarsely croaked, as he lay on his deathbed, at the age of ninety-three. "Build a memorial to the great Winthrop name. Find a good woman to be your wife, to give you sons, so that the Winthrop name shall carry on through

2

eternity." He then took his last breath and was no more.

As luck would have it, a mere week later, Randolph The First bumped, that's right, literally bumped into his forthcoming bride, Mildred. The young lass of eighteen, was coming out of a grocery store, when the grieving Randolph, tears still fogging his sight from the loss of his grandfather, not looking where he was going, smacked right into her. She and her bags went flying to the cobbled pavement. Awkwardly helping her up, trying and failing not to stare at the sight of her pretty white pantaloons, he knew right then that he had found the love of his life. Mildred was not so sure.

But Randolph courted her like a prince would, buying her anything her virgin heart might desire, even though the innocent Mildred had no inkling of what a heart should desire in the first place. On the other hand, her father did. "Marry him!" he demanded. "He's wealthy, he's good-looking. He's a Winthrop, for crying out loud! You're almost an old maid, my dear. I can't support you, forever! Marry him!"

And so it came to pass. During their extensive engagement Randolph built for her the great Winthrop Manor. They were married in the grand ballroom on a sunny spring day, as the young weeping willow outside the window swayed gently in the breeze. And she grew to love her new husband, at least, as much as she knew what love was.

Seven months later, the pregnant Mildred doubled over in excruciating pain during an elaborate dinner party at the Manor and hours later, miscarried. Luckily, there was a doctor in the house. It was a boy, he sadly told them. Randolph was beside himself. Mildred, quickly knocked out by ether administered to her by the kind doc, had no idea what had transpired until the next day. Ten months after that, Mildred lost another son, this time in childbirth. It seemed to Mildred that her husband seemed more distressed about the loss of the family name continuing, than the despair she was feeling. What was a woman's, a wife's place on this earth, if not to bear children? And if so, then what was her place on earth? She felt like an utter failure.

But less than one year later, the Winthrop name was saved, that by finally and happily, the healthy birth of Randolph Winthrop The Second. A prince was born and all in the Manor celebrated. The stars in the sky twinkled brighter than ever that night, as the newborn screamed at the top of his lungs for his now, milk-maid mother to spew forth his sustenance. As the years rolled on, although Mildred tried and tried to give her husband, hopefully, another son, it was not to be. In the deepest recesses of her soul, Mildred longed for a little girl, but that was not to be, either. Randolph Winthrop The Second grew up an only-child, spoiled in the luxury smothered unto him by his father. This turned out to be a good and lucky thing, due to the fact that Randolph The Second didn't happen to be born the brightest bulb on the block. Perhaps, a candle without a wick, might be more accurate.

By the mid 1920's, horse thieving and dog racing wasn't as lucrative as it once had been and gambling had become too much of a gamble, so Randolph The First set his sights higher. He had a Manor, a wife and a twenty-something son to maintain. Randolph The Second had no desire to leave home or do much of anything. He enjoyed living off his father and lectures by his mother to make something of himself, fell into the deep crevice between his ears. On the plus side, he could do a mean Charleston.

Surprisingly and quite accidentally, it was Randolph The Second who got his father into a new business. Out one night at an underground party, he met Jack Danton, a writer whose great American novel was only one break away. He fancied himself to be the next F. Scott Fitzgerald, whose The Great Gatsby had recently been published. To make money to support his literary dreams, Jack hosted small gatherings where bootlegged booze was served. Considering Prohibition was in full swing, this meant having some shady pals in the gangster world. When Jack learned who Randolph The Second's father was, he took the opportunity to offer him a deal he could hardly refuse.

And so began the infamous Winthrop Manor's "underground" liquor-filled parties, that were common knowledge around town. Everyone who was anyone in greater Los Angeles came... movie stars, directors, producers, politicians, the crème de la crème of Hollywood society. And why not? The surroundings were grand, the drinks, excellent, the food divine and the bands so very danceable. The Police Chief and even the Mayor were known to cut a rug in the Grand Ballroom on those not-so-secret nights. Randolph The First was now rolling in money, Jack was living high off the hog and Randolph The Second felt like a success with the 2% his father gave him off the 'door's' earnings. Oh, yes, it wasn't cheap to get invited to the great Winthrop Manor. And the liquor-filled gravy train for Jack and the Winthrop's went on for a number of years.

It was also dangerous, what with gun-toting gangsters vying for the best territory in the city to make more loot. The Winthrop Manor was becoming a fortress, guarded by high-paid thugs, day and night. And Mildred hated it. More than once, she had heard whispers about a 'Benny The Blimp' and how there was revenge in his heart. But she had no idea exactly who he was or what that meant.

"We have enough money, Randolph One," she pleaded. "I hate my house being used this way! And I'm scared that something bad is going to happen."

"Have no fear, my Dear." Randolph One said, as he gently put a new, large diamond pendant around her neck, "Nothing bad is going to happen. And you do so like what our parties reap, don't you? Ah, that looks so beautiful around your lovely, lily-white neck."

Mildred admired her new bauble in the mirror. "Thank you, Randolph One. It's lovely."

Yes, yes, Mildred did enjoy her expensive jewelry and furs and gowns. But besides having this ominous feeling in her gut, something inside of her also seemed so dead. And every now and again she wondered, Who am I? Why am I here? What is love? Is this what life is all about? Is this all there is? But then, as the reveler strangers started to fill up her house, Randolph One whisked her away for a sumptuous dinner at the famous Coconut Grove or some other expensive eatery.

And then life changed, drastically, for everyone. First there was the big shoot out, but that's for a later chapter. Then it was the Stock Market Crash of '29. Too many of the oh-so-rich folks weren't oh-so-rich, anymore and even Hollywood was suffering. Besides not being able to afford a party at the Winthrop Manor, much less anything else, no one was in the mood to celebrate, to say the least. They were busy looking for a window to jump out of. And many of them found one. Randolph The First lost a bundle in the Crash, but Mildred suspected he had been hiding bills under one of the mattresses in one of the Manor's fifteen bedrooms, because as the Great Depression spread over the country like a dastardly plague, their lives didn't change all that much.

On the other hand, investing in the Market through the years, thinking he would make a killing and finally really proving himself to his father as an upstanding citizen, Randolph The Second lost everything his father had given to him. At least he still had a very large roof over his head. And a new bride, Cassandra. Mildred quickly realized that the new Mrs. Randolph The Second did not, necessarily, marry for love, at all, but for money she thought was in abundance. The truth was, Cassandra, a wanna-be actress, had no idea that her new husband was actually broke and being supported by his father, totally and completely. Would she have cared, had she'd known? Doubtful. On her own and almost broke, what she did know was that she was now living in a manner she would have never dreamed possible. Perhaps it was a good thing she married, Randolph The Second, or anyone, at that point in her life, since her acting skills certainly lacked. A Lillian Gish, she wasn't. As a thank you for her new living arrangements, her new lease on life, she quickly presented the family with Randolph Winthrop The Third. But try as she might, as the years passed by, she was unable to give to the family a Randolph The Forth, or Fifth, for that matter. It seemed to be one wife, one son for the Winthrop dynasty and that was all.

As Randolph the First wheeled and dealed, made money, lost some, made some more, even becoming a movie producer of little to no prominence, Mildred seemed to fade away into her own little world. She was more of a mother to her grandson than was Cassandra a mother. Years later, when Randolph The Third grew up and married Teresa, a club singer, Mildred patiently waited for a great-grandchild to be born, hopefully a little girl, this time, so she could then, again, mother, because that was the only thing she seemed to know how to do, although she wasn't even sure she was very good at that.

Growing up, Randolph Winthrop The Third was an odd egg, his grandfather believed. As a child, 'The Third', as he was sometimes referred to, reminded his grandfather of the stories he had heard about his own father, Rudolph Winthrop The Sixth. The Third seemed always to be in his own little world, talking to himself, constantly drawing strange pictures of fairies and goblins, putting on one person shows in front of the mirror. He seemed to care nothing at all about the trappings that surrounded him. Of course, Mildred had a soft spot in her heart for this seemingly otherworldly creature. Unfortunately, feeling as if he had been born into the wrong family, he started drinking when he was in high school. His father, Randolph The Second, basically ignored him, as, sadly, did his mother.

When he was twenty-one, his trust kicked in. With the money, he bought all kinds of musical equipment, drums, cymbals, an accordion, a kazoo and more and set up his self-made one man band on corner of Hollywood and Vine. He was very proud of the nickels and dimes people threw in his hat. Sometimes while playing, he would also read his deeply personal poems for all to hear. Of course, he was drunk all the time, so he thought all the clapping and laughing by the people passing by was a compliment to his musical and poetic virtuosity.

It was, in fact, on this historic corner that he met Teresa, his future wife. She fell in love with him by first poem. Being a wanna-a-be chanteuse, sometimes she would sing his poems, as he blew his kazoo. It was a match made in Hollywood, that's for sure.

By the 1950's, it was obvious that the great Winthrop Manor was not what it used to be. The foundation seemed to be quickly decaying, as were the inhabitants who lived inside of it. Mildred begged Randolph One to sell the old fossil, demand their entire live-in family move the hell out and finally fend for themselves, but Randolph One refused.

"I built this Manor for you, Millie. It's our family's legacy. I promised my grand-pappy. I'll die before I sell it! And I swear to you, I'll come back from the grave if the Winthrop Manor ever leaves this family!"

As the years continued to roll on, now closing in on eighty, Randolph One was spending more and more time at different movie studios, hoping to get funding for his newest B minus, minus horror flick, strutting around the lot's Commissary, true, with a cane, pretending to be some Hollywood hotshot, when he met a pretty young thing, an extra with big dreams of being yet another Marilyn Monroe, waiting with baited breath to be discovered. Smelling money and the possibility of fame, she became his little coquette, giving him the love and attention that Mildred didn't even pretend to give him, anymore.

When Mildred caught wind of this relationship, through a gossipy friend, who happened to be lunching at the studio and spied the old man and young thing kissing in front of a fake bar on a western set, she was so disgusted, she just had to spew the truth. And that was the straw that broke the camel's back. Mildred made the bold move out of the Manor to strike, well, at her age, hobble, out on her own.

Randolph was devastated, but gave her money, without her asking, to rent a lovely, but small little apartment in Beverly Hills. Once the sweet young thing learned there was no money, no fame, no anything to be gained from extolling all that affection on this smelly old man, she disappeared from his life. This news did not bring Mildred home. She kept herself busy by crocheting colorful doilies and baby bonnets and socks, actually selling them at a local knick-knack store around the corner from her apartment.

She only saw her husband of close to sixty years two more times after that. The first was when the still strange, now adult Randolph The Third married Teresa. It was an awkward afternoon, to say the least. They married in a park, under a tree, with a Justice Of The Peace officiating. They sang love poems to each other as their vows. It was quite sweet. But Mildred was hardly even cordial to her estranged husband, as he tried his best to woo her back, with absolutely no luck.

Less than a year later, Teresa presented to the family, Randolph Winthrop The Fourth. A month after that, Randolph Winthrop The First, son of Rudolph Winthrop The Sixth, grandson of Rudolph Winthrop The Fifth, lay dying in the now faded master bedroom of what once was the great Winthrop Manor. And this was the second time Mildred saw her husband since she had left him for his terrible indiscretion.

The land around the Manor was dying, too, had been dying for a long, long time. The grass was like straw for lack of watering. The green ivy that once climbed the Manor's walls had for too long become nothing but dead tendrils. And outside the grand ballroom, the weeping willow, now huge, but aching for the sky's liquid, seemed to weep for her surroundings that were no more, for seemingly the end of an era.

In the master bedroom, the smell of death was breathed in by family members. They all

13

stood around the huge bed, Randolph Two and Three, their respected wives, Cassandra and Teresa and in her arms, the newest Winthrop, Randolph The Fourth. And Mildred.

Frail and with labored breath, Randolph The First seemed to go in and out of consciousness. Mildred looked to the man she had married so long ago, then her eyes drifted over to the bed stand and the framed sepia-toned photograph taken on their wedding day, standing in front of the newly-built Manor. How young they looked. He looked ecstatic. She looked, well, happy. He had promised her a wonderful life that day. He had promised her he would love her, forever.

Now she looked at the corpse of a man in their wedding bed of so long ago and wondered where the years had gone. And had it been a wonderful life? And had she ever really been happy? And had all her dreams been fulfilled? And had she really ever had any dreams at all?

His eyes fluttered open, landing on Mildred's sweet, now wrinkled face.

"Mildred... my Millie... You've come back to me," his voice, barely a whisper.

Mildred stared at this once strapping, now shell of a man, wearing his favorite striped pajamas. "No, Randolph One. I've come to see you off…" In her heart, she didn't mean for it to come out so harshly. But it did.

"Mother!" That from Randolph The Second. "Father's dying, for crying out loud. Can't you just make up? Can't you just give him that? Especially now?"

Cassandra, his wife, had to put in her two sense. "Yes, Mother Winthrop. Isn't it time to put your… differences aside, whatever they were in the first place?" And she burst into tearless tears. "He's… he's not long for this world, for goodness sake. Such a wonderful man…"

Anger rose up in Mildred. "Ah, yes, Cassandra. Suddenly sympathetic words from the always greedy daughter-in-law. Only there's not much left to be greedy about, now, is there?"

"Please, Grandmother, must we fight, today of all days?" slurred Randolph The Third. He was drunk as usual.

"This isn't any of your business, Randolph Three. And isn't it a tad early for you to be drinking?" Cassandra blurted out.

In response, Randolph The Third, let out a large, loud burp.

Mildred looked over what she considered her dysfunctional family. "Oh, if you knew the real truth about this family…"

Suddenly Randolph The First moaned a deep moan. "Millie... My Millie. I always loved you... always.

"No, Randolph One, I'm afraid what you really loved was money and what money could buy. You loved this decaying piece of cement, more than you loved me." Mildred waved and waved her arms all around the room. "And now it's all faded, just like you. Just like you."

"But I did it for you, my Darling. For you... everything was for you...'

Now Mildred felt even angrier and oh, so tired. "And you lost it. You lost it all. The money. Me. And for what? Look what you did, Randolph One. Look what you...." She started to say something about the real truth of why she had left him, how he had cheated on her, with nothing more than a little, ambitious whore! A tramp, who just like all the others, even her children, were only out for his money. "That's not what I wanted! Not what I really wanted..."

Surprising everyone, Randolph One bolted upright. "Then what?" he said, his voice momentarily stronger. "What did you want... my Millie...?" He looked at her with such yearning, desperation and love in his tearing eyes. Then just as she began to try and answer him, he fell back onto his pillows, took one last gasp of breath, closed his eyes and died.

"Grandpa!! Grandpa," screamed his drunk grandson. "Don't leave."

Baby Randolph The Fourth, all of two months old, wriggled in his mother's arms and let out a screeching wail!

Son, daughter-in-law, great-granddaughter-in-law all drew closer to the death bed, not believing the beloved patriarch was really gone, secretly hoping there was a secret will leaving them hidden millions. Only Randolph Three looked truly heartbroken.

No one seemed to notice that Mildred hadn't moved closer to the bed, as they had. Even with all her anger toward her husband, no one thought to put their arms around her, to comfort her. But she wasn't surprised. Sixty years, she thought. She gazed over to Randolph The First. Suddenly he looked peaceful, his pain finally gone. Her eyes then again drifted to her wedding photo on the bed stand. And had any of her little family been paying attention to her, they would have seen her pain. They would have seen her tears.

Suddenly and out of nowhere, one of the windows in the room flew open and a strong gust of wind entered the room.

Five years later, to the day her husband left this earth, Mildred, who had moved back into the

Manor, died, also. Her family, whom she had made a vague peace with, stood near to her, as she sat in her favorite chair in the master bedroom. Moments before she ceased to exist on this earthly plane, she looked out the open window at the great weeping willow.

"Randolph One, are you there? Are you there?" she softly called out.

Her family was sure that the poor woman had been instantly felled with dementia and hoped her suffering would soon end. It did. She leaned back in the chair and drew her last breath. It was 1965 and the Viet Nam War was still raging. But Mildred would rage no more in this life.

CHAPTER TWO

JACK AND SUSANNA

From the day Jack Danton was born, he was a charmer. "This boy could charm a snake," exclaimed his mother, proudly. "In fact, he charmed his big brother's pants right off him for his senior dance!" she laughed.

Adorable from birth, so handsome as a young man, Jack just knew in his heart he was destined for great things. He had dreams, big dreams. And he seemingly had the talent to back up those dreams. From an early age, he knew it would be through the written word that his dreams would materialize into reality. Once he learned his alphabet, he began to write. And

19

what an imagination the young boy had. He wrote stories about horses that could fly, chipmunks who took over the world, inanimate objects that were alive. And even at such a tender age, his stories always had a beginning, middle and end, developed characters and a satisfying resolution. A genius, thought his mother. His father saw his boy's talent, but was disappointed he wouldn't be the next generation to run the farm. Jack made the decision early on, that that could be left to his big brother, who loved herding the cows and feeding the pigs. He had bigger fish to fry and they weren't swimming in the near-by lake.

The 1920's were starting to roar and Jack felt the need to go where the action was and the action certainly wasn't in the small Midwestern town he was born in. Go west, young man, go west, said the voice inside his head. And so he bid a fond farewell to his family and with a few bucks stuffed in his pocket by his loving mother, he hitchhiked his way to where the stars glittered and there was gold in them there hills. Unfortunately, much of the gold had already been mined.

Finding work that would pay his bills wasn't as easy as he thought. He scooped ice cream at an ice cream parlor, slung hash at a cheap diner, even shined shoes at the train station, all the while writing about the sights and sounds of his chosen town of dreams.

Finally, he lucked out and got a job at the Los Angeles Times. Unfortunately, it was in the sports department, something he had little to no interest in writing about. While he toiled during the day over stories about Babe Ruth hitting another home run or Jack Dempsey fighting and losing to Gene Tunney or Caroline Gertrude Ederte swimming across the English Channel, he went home each night to his dingy downtown hovel to work on what he knew in his heart would be the next great American novel.

At work, although girls were always batting their eyelashes at him, raising their skirts a little higher as they sat at their secretary desks, he was like a horse with blinders on. He would get published, become a literary sensation and then have time for real romance, real love. That is not to say he hadn't danced his way with a number of the fairer sex. No, Jack was never at a loss for female companionship. But he did have scruples. Never, ever date anyone in the workplace. He had tried it once and it was a disaster. The poor girl, destroyed when he broke up with her, couldn't do her work and was fired. Never again, he promised himself.

All went according to plan, that is, until he laid his eyes on the beautiful baby blues of a new secretary to the Home Section editor of the paper. She was different from the rest. Her skirt was longer, a beret was always perched on her head, half covering her brown bobbed locks and most of all, she never gave Jack a first glance, a mere hint that she might want to get to know him.

She was the beautiful Susanna Kolinsky. A Jew, born in the little town of Odessa, Russia, she came to the states when she was ten months old, bundled in her mother's arms, in the bowels of a freighter ship, as her father fled the Czar's army. Her parents were Communists, fighting for the rights of the common folk. Landing first in New York, then moving to Chicago, her mother was a suffragette, marching for women's rights. The poor woman would have turned over in her grave, had she not have been cremated when she died, had she known how many years it had actually taken for women to be considered somewhat equal.

As Susanna grew up, like her parents, she made it her life's effort to fight the good fight for a better world, equality for all humankind, better wages, working conditions, sharing of the wealth and all the things that went along with being a good little, now American Communist. After her parents early deaths, she migrated to Los Angeles, where she went to union meetings, walked picket lines, distributed leaflets, always fighting the 'man' on behalf of the little people, the workers. But that did not pay the bills and so she ended up a secretary at the Los Angeles Times.

On a rare rainy day in the sunshine state, Jack took a deep breath and sauntered up to Susanna's perfectly organized desk.

"Why do you hate me, pretty lady?" he asked with all the cuteness he could muster.

Susanna didn't look up at him. "First of all, I don't hate you, because I don't know you to hate you. And second of all, I am not a lady!"

"Really!" he laughed.

She didn't. "No! Being called that is an insult in my book. I'm a woman! Not a lady, not a babe, not a girl! A woman!"

It was rare for Jack to be at a loss for words, especially with the... ladies, but this was one of those times. "Oh..." was all he could come up with. Then... "Oh....," again.

He walked away with his tail between his legs and missed seeing her smile slightly, as she buried her head back into her work. Oh yes, she had noticed him before, as he strolled around the huge newsroom, flirting with all the 'girls' in his confident, arrogant manner.

Three days later, he got up the gumption to try again. Hesitantly, he walked up to her desk.

"Ahh... can we start again? I'm humbly sorry. Will you accept my apology? Pretty please, pretty... woman?"

Susanna looked up from her desk and laughed. "Well... okay. Apology accepted." They looked into each other's eyes and so began their love affair.

Within months they were living together in the quaint little cottage she rented at the base of the Hollywood Hills. She thought he was a brilliant writer and he thought she was just brilliant. They talked nights in front of a blazing fire, sipping cheap wine, of his dreams of becoming a great and distinguished writer and her work of changing the world for the better. And the two of them believed their love was the ultimate love. And it was, for a while, at least.

Speaking of cheap wine, since Prohibition was the law of the land, Jack had some friends, especially one in the name of Hank Harris, a small-time thug and bootlegger who supplied Jack and some of the other editors at work with liquor. He was also into having small gambling evenings. No, he was no Al Capone, but he made a damn good living, much more than Jack did, slaving away writing about a subject he had absolutely no interest in.

And so it was, one night when Susanna was out fighting for people's rights, Hank convinced Jack to come to one of his gambling soirees. By the end of the evening Jack had swallowed more whisky than he should have and had somehow won three hundred dollars playing poker.

"I'm impressed, Jack. Didn't know you were such a player."

"Ah, beginner's luck," Jack slurred. "But this is great. I just made, in three hours, more than I do working months at the paper."

Hank thought a moment. "Well, my friend, I like you, so I'm gonna tell you how I'm gonna help you make ten times that much in a day."

"I'm listening." Jack's eyes opened wide in anticipation.

And so it began, a new profession for Jack Danton. A new 'job' that would give Jack a chance to work more on his writing while not worrying about money. And charming Jack was very, very good at what he did. Within weeks, he had set up more gambling parties than Hank did in a month. Being the new, successful kid, on the block, bootleggers were falling over themselves to make deals with him, supplying his parties with booze. But Los Angeles was a small town and one had to be very careful not to over-step one's boundaries, one's territory.

Jack had been warned about a gangster named Benny Marcello, known to everyone who was anyone as Benny The Blimp. Yes, he was a fat slob of a guy and he packed heat, a lot of heat. The problem with Benny was that he thought all of Southern California was his territory. He didn't care about small timers like Hank, but if anyone got too successful, then he took it upon himself to shut them down, shut down forever! But Jack wasn't worried, since in his heart, he knew doing this kind of work was simply a short-time means to an end for him, an opportunity to finish his great American novel.

Susanna hated Jack's new vocation and told him so. They argued about it constantly, but she softened just a bit when she saw his happiness at being able to write, full time.

And then at one of his gambling parties, in strolled Randolph Winthrop The Second. Jack thought the guy was a dim bulb, until he learned who his father was and then it hit him. He had heard about the Winthrop Manor and an idea of grand proportions swirled around in his head. A meeting was planned between Jack and Randolph Winthrop The First, introductions were made and a deal was struck.

Within weeks after meeting with Randolph One, the first grand party at the Winthrop Manor was planned. And what a party it was. Word got around Hollywood quickly that this was the place to be for great food, dancing and especially the best liquor in town. Jack would split the 'door', 50/50 with old man Winthrop and they all would get rich. And so they did. At first the parties were held once a month, but the thirst for the Hollywood crowd to mingle and eat and drink in relative obscurity, away from the prying eyes of reporters and photographers, became a weekly happening. And Jack quickly became the man of the hour.

Randolph Winthrop The First was so delighted with the swell of money filling his pockets, that when Jack and Susanna decided to marry, he planned to throw them an extravagant wedding in the Grand Ballroom.

"But I don't want to be married there, Jack!" complained Susanna, loudly. "I just pictured us going down to City Hall, then maybe driving up the coast to Santa Barbara for a little honeymoon. I'm not that kind of person. We're not that kind of people. And truthfully, everything Winthrop stands for, I hate."

Jack finally convinced her how hurt Randolph One would be. It was a thank you, for all the 'good people' Jack had brought to the Manor, he explained to her. It would be so rude to say no. But he promised her the honeymoon of her choice and reminded her of how he was already thinking about his second novel, having now had the opportunity to finish his first great tome. A means to an end, he repeated to her every chance he could. And hadn't old man Winthrop promised to introduce him to a man who knew a man who knew a literary agent?

The big day came and while Susanna was putting on her simple white dress in one of the many Manor bedrooms, Mildred entered.

"You look lovely, Dear. But are you sure you don't want to wear one of my diamond necklaces? Something borrowed, you know," asked Mildred.

Susanna looked at the sweet woman but turned her down. "No, Mrs. Winthrop, I'm wearing my mother's pearls. She left them to me. They mean a lot to me. But thank you so much. And thank you for throwing us this beautiful wedding. I never imagined being married in a place like this, that's for sure."

"I was married here, too, you know. Almost thirty years ago. Randolph One built this... place for me. I didn't need, nor want such a big house, but there's no arguing with your husband-to-be, is there?"

Susanna noticed a sadness in Mildred's eyes. "No, I guess not."

"My, my where did the years go?" Mildred went on, almost dreamily. "But you and Jack are just beginning your journey and I'm sure it will be a wonderful one."

"I hope so."

Susanna thought Mildred to be such a sad soul. Here she was living in the lap of luxury and still not seemingly to be very happy. But she knew the truth. She worked for the truth. It was not money that brought happiness, it was the self-worth that comes from making a difference in other people's lives. She wondered if Mildred ever thought of such things.

And the years rolled by. Susanna still worked for the Times and continued her organizing and picketing, but it seemed like the world was not becoming a better place. All the while, Jack got more and more involved in his gambling parties and holding court at the Winthrop Manor. And all the while, Benny The Blimp was watching. And waiting. And plotting.

On their three year anniversary, Jack surprised his wife with a huge party at the Winthrop Manor. She had only been there once before, on her wedding day. Unfortunately, it wasn't really an anniversary party, at all, but yet another weekend Winthrop gala.

Susanna was instantly uncomfortable at all the gangster-looking goons with guns at every door. Wearing her simple skirt and sweater, her beret on top of her now longer bob, she felt like a fish out of water next to all the girls with so much make-up, wearing fancy flapper dresses and high heels. She stood alone in the corner, wondering where her husband of three years was.

All things considered it had been a good three years, despite the fact that Jack seemed to write less and less, spending more and more time with men of questionable means. But she loved him and she knew he loved her. Sure he was dressing in a more flamboyant way and yes he had bought a gun that he wore in a shoulder holster whenever he was hosting yet another of his 'parties' and she hated that. But don't all couples quarrel, every now and again? It was just that this night, she would have so much rather have been home alone with him, cozy and content in front of a fire, talking about literature and life, like they used to. And suddenly she was feeling very angry at him, at being there, at the way all those flappers kept flirting with him whenever he sauntered by them.

She finally spotted him at the long hand-carved wood bar, drinking with some men. She watched as the men shook Jack's hand and left. Then she saw Jack wave at Randolph One and Mildred at the door. With Mildred, dressed in a long fur coat and Randolph in a tux, it was obvious to Susanna they weren't staying for her anniversary party.

She finally got Jack's attention, by waving. Somewhat drunk, he weaved over to her.

"What ya doing, baby? C'mon, let's dance! It's our anniversary!"

She looked him straight in the eye. "I don't want to dance, Jack. I don't want to be here. I want to go home!"

"Go home? Whatta ya mean, it's our anniversary. C'mon, let's dance." And he tried to pull her onto the dance floor where couples were doing the Charleston to the live band.

But Susanna stood her ground. "I don't want to dance, Jack!"

He tried to kiss her, but she moved her head away from his lips.

"What's the matter with you? Do you know how much I paid for this party. Randolph didn't give it to me for free, ya know!"

Now Susanna was really angry. "Who are you kidding, Jack? This is just another one of your bootlegged parties! You and Winthrop will probably make a fortune, tonight!"

"No, no, it's our anniversary party. Three years ago I married my sweetheart, the love of my life, right here in this room. Isn't that romantic? C'mon! Let the celebration begin!"

Jack was drunk and Susanna hated when he drank so much.

"Celebrate what, Jack? You said you weren't going to do this anymore. You've made enough money to live a good long while without working. You promised me you'd get out of this racket! And when did you forget about your writing? You haven't written a word in I don't know how long."

"But I'm doing this for you, baby, for you."

"For me?" She was almost screaming now. "I don't even know these people. I should be with my comrades now and not here!"

"What, picketing some Woolworth's for better wages? You're gonna end up in jail one of these day, ya know?"

"And you're not?! I'd rather go to jail for a good cause than providing bootlegged booze for a bunch of rich drunks! I'm telling you, Jack, if the Feds don't get you then Benny The Blimp will!"

The look on Jack's face was of total surprise. "What do you know about Benny The Blimp?"

"I'm not stupid, Jack. I hear things. And I'm afraid. I'm begging you to quit now, before it's too late." She was almost in tears, now.

Jack gently took her face in his hands and softy kissed her lips. "Don't you worry your pretty little face about anything, okay? Look around. This place is guarded better then the cons at Alcatraz."

Sure enough, every door to the Grand Ballroom was guarded by men holding machine guns at the ready.

And then, before Susanna could utter another word, the Ballroom doors busted open. A tough bunch of gangsters pushed through the crowd, led by the infamous Benny The Blimp.

All activity suddenly stopped, then everyone started running for cover. It was sheer mayhem. Benny The Blimp looked around the room, then saw Jack.

"Hey, Jack the Rat! We finally meet! I told ya to stay the hell out of my territory! But you didn't listen, did ya?"

The truth was, Benny had know for a long time about Jack and Winthrop and the parties, but had been in Chicago doing some work for Capone for a couple of years. But he was back now and out for vengeance. He hadn't realized what a success Jack had become. Since The Blimp hadn't shown his face for a while, Jack and his cronies thought the big man might be dead. Well, he wasn't.

"Now you're a dead man," Benny The Blimp spewed forth.

Suddenly machine guns started going off in all directions. People started running every which way, ducking under tables, anything to stay alive. Rat-a-tat-tat. The sound went on and on and on. And then it stopped. Benny The Blimp looked smug as he signaled for his gang to leave.

And there in the corner, blood spattered over their now dead bodies, lay Jack and Susanna, in each other's arms.

CHAPTER THREE

JIMMY AND HEATHER

It was the early 1970's and on the great lawn of the now completely deteriorated Winthrop Manor a 'Happening' was happening, your typical anti-war love in, or a place for a bunch of hippies to do nothing but get high as kites.

Randolph The First was long gone, as was Mildred. Randolph The Second, having had a massive heart attack, was gone, too. His wife, Cassandra, having been left nothing, because there was nothing left to leave, that she knew of, had quickly found a rich tycoon to keep her in furs and jewels. And so it was that only

35

Randolph The Third, now in his fifties, was left the honor of maintaining the Great Winthrop Manor. He failed. Teresa, his wife, had left him when the money dried up, taking their young son, Randolph Winthrop The Fourth, with her. And so Randolph The Third was all alone, rattling around the cold corridors of what once was that beacon of ostentatious glamour overlooking the City Of Angels. But that was a long, long time ago.

It was the era of love beads and hippy garb and "Peace, man," and getting high. High it was that Randolph The Third always seemed to be. And so it came to pass that the Manor became the place to hang, to picnic, to get stoned. Hippies came from all over, crashing in the once elegant bedrooms, planting vegetables in the garden for their nourishment, singing songs of peace, making the Manor their own commune, high in the hills of Hollywood.

Young braless women with flowers in their hair, wearing long flowing skirts, tended to their babies and young men with just lots of hair, wearing tie-dye shirts and ripped jeans roamed the property. The Age Of Aquarius was alive and well at Winthrop Manor.

The large parking area was filled with V. W. vans and 'beetles' and other old cars covered with painted flowers and peace slogans, as well as a number of motorcycles.

On one particular Sunday, on a ratty old blanket, sat Heather and Jimmy, both in their early twenties. They were listening to a folk group singing anti-war songs on a make-shift stage. They were both children of Southern California, high school sweethearts who a year before had married under the huge weeping willow, near to the place they now sat.

The lovely, long-flowing haired Heather McGuire was a girl of serious nature. Having recently graduated UCLA and going for her Masters in Political Science, she had not yet decided exactly what she wanted to do with her life. Adamantly against the Viet Nam war, she did know that she wanted to do something of consequence, make the world a better place for all people, not that unlike Susanna had, over forty years before. Heather came from a stable, liberal family, her parents both social workers. They didn't have a lot of money, but they had good hearts.

She and the adorable Jimmy Callen had fallen in love in the eleventh grade at Hollywood High School. Her house was a refuge for him, the only child of divorced parents and Heather's mother and father adored him and treated him like their own.

From an early age it was obvious that Jimmy had talent. A terrific singer, was he, always landing the solos in his high school glee club. While still in school, he formed a barbershop quartet and sang at school parties. Teaching himself the guitar and writing his own songs, he had big dreams of one day soon having a band the likes of The Eagles or Crosby, Stills and Nash. He longed to snag a recording deal, to headline at the famous, newly opened 'Roxy' on the Sunset Strip, to hobnob with Jackson Browne and Neil Young. In the meantime, to pay the rent and help put Heather through school, he worked for the phone company, climbing poles, all the while song ideas humming in his head.

Hanging out at the Winthrop Manor wasn't one of Heather's favorite things to do. She might have been a hippy in looks, but not really in spirit. She went there, mainly, for Jimmy, who sang for the stoned crowd every chance he could, hoping that maybe, maybe, some person with ties to the record industry might be out scouting for the next Cat Stevens or James Taylor.

She agreed to be married on the Manor's lawn under the weeping willow because even she had to admit it was a peaceful, beautiful place to wed, not to mention there was no way she wanted to make her parents use all their money on one day, special as it was.

On a beautiful, warm spring day, Jimmy and Heather started their life together as husband and wife, both with their own dreams, hers to help others, his to help himself.

And so it was on another balmy, sunny, southern California spring day, one year later, a rather buzzed Jimmy, doing riffs on his guitar and a not buzzed at all Heather, sat on that old blanket, nibbling on grapes and cheese, when an old, by their young standards, bearded, completely zoned out hippy approached them. It was Randolph The Third.

"Hey man, peace, ya know what I mean?" Randolph Three said, as he held his favorite bong.

"I know what you mean, Randolph Three," answered Jimmy, while Heather busied herself peeling a grape.

"Yeah, groovy time. You diggin' it, Jimmy, my man?"

"Groovin' and diggin' it."

"Yeah... cool... cool... Yeah, man... Hey, Jimmy's chick, you groovin' and diggin' it?"

Heather looked up at the sad old man. "Yeah, Three, that's what I'm doing," she said with a sarcastic edge to her voice that both men missed.

"Yeah, that's good, Jimmy's chick. Yeah... you keep doin'... that... Here, man, from me to you." And then, after dropping in Jimmy's lap a plastic bag filled with weed, Randolph The Third wandered away.

Jimmy opened the bag and took a sniff. "Mm, good stuff."

"You didn't pay for that, did you?" questioned Heather.

"No, baby, it was a gift."

"For what?"

"I dunno. For just being. Being here, playing and singing for the crowd. I dunno." Jimmy took a hit off his joint, then tried to pass it to Heather. She declined.

"C'mon, Honey, it's good stuff."

"I told you I have a big test, tomorrow. I've got to keep my head clear. How much longer are we going to stay, Jimmy? I want to go home and study."

"I haven't sung, yet, Baby. I heard some of David Geffen's guys might show up. Do you know what it would mean to get on his record label?"

Heather sighed deeply, laid down on the blanket and started looking through her backpack. She figured if she had to hang there around all day, she might as well get some studying done and was glad she had remembered to take her books. But Jimmy would have none of it. He took the book out of her hands and laid himself on top of her, kissing her passionately.

"Jimmy!"

"What? I can't kiss my wife?"

"Why don't you go up and sing, then we can go home."

"I have a better idea," Jimmy said as he tried kissing her again. "Let's us make ourselves a baby!"

"What, right here?" Heather had to laugh.

"Why not?"

Heather looked around the grounds. Couples were actually making love, behind bushes, even out in the open. The place looked like Woodstock without all the mud.

"C'mon, Heather, we gotta do our part to populate this country with more folks like us, right? Make up for all those idiots who are sending kids to get killed in Nam, for nothing, right?" There was passion and anger in his voice. "All the good guys are dead. JFK and Bobby and Martin. You're always talkin' about making this world a better place and this is a way to do it." He again tried to kiss her, but to no avail.

"I don't want to have a kid in this world, not the way it is! When we have kids, hopefully he or she will grow up in a world where there won't be any more wars and hate."

Angry, now, Jimmy rolled off his wife. "Dream on, baby, dream on. War and domination over others is human nature, man. The worst of human nature. I'll bet in thirty years there will still be wars and hate and killings of innocent lives. And for what? For nothing, that's for what."

Idealist that Heather was, she wouldn't believe that and responded angrily. "No, Jimmy! Not if we do something great, now. Maybe if you stopped smoking so much dope and *did* something of consequence, instead of just complain..."

Hurt, he interrupted her. "Hey, I bring home the bacon, I'm putting you through school. You think I like climbing those god-damn poles for the damn phone company? And I do, do something! I sing at marches and stuff and one day my music is gonna help change the world... if someone would just give me a break..."

"Songs can't change the world, Jimmy," she said, now more softly. "Action changes things. I've been seriously thinking I might get into politics after I get my Masters. That's the way to really have my voice heard."

"And maybe be silenced... forever." Jimmy took another toke off his joint. "Anyway, politics is the most corrupt world there is."

"Then why would I want to bring a baby into this crappy world, anyway? Tell me that!"

Now Jimmy was fuming. "So, what're you saying? We're never gonna have kids?"

"I didn't say that. Just not now!"

One thing Jimmy always had had a soft spot in his heart for was kids. When he was young he used to baby-sit the neighbor's children. First he did it just to have a couple of bucks in his pocket, but to him, there was something about little ones he just loved. Their soft smell. The way they fell asleep on his lap while he was singing them lullabies. Jimmy was just crazy about little ones.

"Damn, Heather, when we were married right here, not a couple of feet away, right here on this lawn a year ago, you knew, you knew how much I wanted kids!"

"I'll have kids, Jimmy! I'll have them when I'm good and ready and I'm not ready right now!"

Pissed, Jimmy stood up, quickly, suddenly dizzy from a sudden rush. "Yeah, right. When you're ready. And when will that be, Heather…?" He started singing the Beatles hit. "… 'When you're sixty-four?' Well, maybe I won't love you anymore…"

And then Jimmy started running toward the parking area. Heather, sadly, watched him go.

She hated fighting with him and the truth was, in all the years they had been together, they hardly ever fought and if they did it was only about him smoking too much, sometimes, or about having or not having children.

Suddenly feeling badly about their fight, Heather jumped up and started running after him, yelling for him to stop, to come back to her, to wait for her. She reached the parking area just as Jimmy jumped on his hog and revered up the motor, loudly. As he started to roar off, she jumped on, behind him.

"C'mon, Jimmy, let's talk about this, okay? You know how much I love you."

Jimmy would have none of it. "What's to talk about, Heather? You've made yourself perfectly clear to me."

His cycle started to move.

"C'mon, Honey, don't. You're too stoned to drive."

Ignoring her, he burned rubber and took off. Heather held on for dear life as Jimmy weaved his heavy machine through the hippy gathering, like a maniac. People started scattering for their lives.

"Jimmy! Jimmy, stop! You're going to kill someone," Heather yelled over the loud din of the engine.

But Jimmy didn't heed her words, recklessly continuing driving through the scared crowd. And then, suddenly, Jimmy lost control of his two-wheel machine and it careened into the huge, unsuspecting weeping willow, right at the very spot where only a year before the two had pledged to love each other 'til death do they part.

As one of the cycle's wheels continued to turn, turn, turn, all the hippies came running, gathering around the scene to view the carnage. The love-in was over. Thrown off to the side lay Jimmy and Heather, bloodied and dead, her arms still tightly hugging his now broken body.

CHAPTER FOUR

<u>RANDOLPH THE FOURTH AND JOSIE</u>

The year was 2003 and after decades of almost total deterioration the Winthrop Manor had been restored to its former glory. Flowers abounded everywhere. The grass was green and once again, healthy ivy crept up the mansion's walls. The weeping willow wept no more.

From his office, on the first floor, conservatively dressed in a suit and tie, which he wore everyday, no matter what the day's agenda might bring, Randolph Winthrop The Fourth, now in his early forties, gazed out over his property. He knew the history of his family and now this house too well. But he could hardly remember ever living there. His mother, Teresa, a rather uptight woman, had divorced his father when he was a mere lad. Once his father, Randolph The Third, got into the drug culture in the mid sixties and remained there until he died, in the early 'me' generation of the eighties, Teresa would not allow the boy to have any contact with him, growing up. She remarried a rich oil man from Dallas a few years after her divorce. Randolph The Fourth went to the best private schools Texas had to offer and grew up the exact opposite of his absent father, a conservative thinking, non-drinking, rather uptight man, not unlike his now-deceased mother had been. His step-father, Buddy, short for Beuford, outlived his beloved Ter-Ter, as he loved to call her, by a number of years. He had raised Randolph The Fourth as his own, giving him everything money could buy.

Once Randolph The Third died, the Winthrop Manor had gone into foreclosure and as a gesture to his lovely Ter-Ter for her son's future, he bought the decaying domicile for a pittance, where for close to twenty years it sat through wind and rain and beating sun, empty, with no one to give it the tender loving care that Randolph Winthrop The First, a century before, had lovingly done.

When Buddy died, Randolph The Fourth, whose mother had always called him Randy, trying to forget the not-so-terrific legacy of the Winthrop's, sat stoically in Buddy's lawyer's office to hear the reading of his will. No one was more surprised than he, to learn that not only had he inherited the Winthrop Manor, but a good chunk of change to go with it. Being the only living descendant of the once great and not-so-great family, it was now up to him to decide what to do with it.

At the time, knowing little of his real father's family history, kept from him by his mother, he now made a concerted effort to learn everything he could about them before deciding what to do. Single, having never finding love and in his late thirties, with nothing to keep him in Texas, he bid a fond farewell to the only home he ever really knew and drove out to Los Angeles in one of his step-father's, now his, Rolls Royce to see for himself.

What he found was a crumbling mess. But as he roamed the decaying halls, he closely peered at the yellowing photographs that lined the walls of the family lost to him. One, that for some reason touched him deeply, was of his whole family, taken right after he was born and only months before his great-grandfather had died. He learned that the only person missing

48

from that photo was his great-grandmother, Mildred.

From the photos and newspaper articles, especially about Randolph The First, he decided what his destiny was. He would restore the Manor and bring back the Winthrop's good name. This was no mean feat, he discovered and it took most of his inheritance to do so. Now he wondered, what he would do. Being a child raised with that proverbial silver spoon in his mouth, he had never really worked. Sure he knew something about the oil business through his step-dad, but he had never really made any kind of living for himself. Pathetic, he thought, now. So much for being taken care of one's whole life. But he was determined to change that. He would do this for himself. He would do this in honor of the man who had built this Manor. That not withstanding, considering how all his life his mother had bad-rapped the family, especially his father and in honor to his mother, he would still only answer to the name, Randy.

After two years of meticulous work, the Manor was ready. Unfortunately, Randy didn't know for what. Also, unfortunately, with money running out and no means to support himself he was starting to feel desperate. And then one night, sitting in a darkened theater, by himself, watching a sappy movie about weddings, it came to him. He would turn the Winthrop Manor into a place of joy and happiness, a place where the wedding of one's dreams could come true. And so it came to pass.

Quickly, life for Randy seemed to be taking a positive turn. Not only were a few nuptials held there, but charity events, Bar and Bat Mitzvahs and the like. Randy even found love in the name of Josie Masters, an adorable woman a few years his junior, who worked at an advertising agency, whom he met while running on a treadmill in one of LA's trendy gyms. After three years of dating, he asked for her hand in marriage. Frustrating for her, he never seemed to get around to asking for the rest of her, nor for her to come and live with him. Knowing how conservative he was concerning social issues such as these, at first she didn't complain. She thought it was sweet, in an old fashioned sort of way. But as happens with most women, her biological clock was ticking and as the months, then years went by, she and it were feeling like rust was setting in.

Yes, Randy wanted to take Josie for his bride, but first he felt he had to really make it and make it big. The truth was, his Winthrop Manor was sucking him dry. The upkeep was enormous and as the days went by, fewer and fewer folks wanted to book the place, especially for weddings and he couldn't figure out why. He had gone to other wedding sites in the city and none compared, came close to what he could offer... the Grand Ballroom, the package deal of the wedding night stay in the perfectly restored master bedroom, the outside property, itself, with its swan filled man-made lake, the rose garden that could give the one at the White House a run for its money. He had turned this place into heaven on earth, the most beautiful venue for a couple in love to start their journey through life together.

The same could be said about what Josie wanted. Josie, for her part, loved Randy. Yes, it was true that her view of the world was much more liberal then his, that his conservative social morays drove her somewhat crazy, but under it all, she understood him and found him to be the sweetest of men. Hell, had she not gone into the advertising field, she believed she would have made a wonderful therapist. She knew his history. For crying out loud, he grew up in Bush's Texas. She had heard all the stories of the dysfunctional Winthrop clan. It didn't take a Freud or a rocket scientist to realize Randy had some psychological work to do on himself. Of course he was adamantly against going to a shrink. 'A real man should be able to figure out his own problems,' he told her one day when she suggested that possibility might be helpful to him. Randolph (Randy) Winthrop The Fourth sometimes reminded Josie of a cross between a man with the brain stuck in the 1950's, inhabiting the body of a man living in the next, new century. But she did love him. It angered her as much as him that as beautiful a place he had made of the Manor, it wasn't as successful as he thought it would be.

Of course, there was the economy. People were already starting to scale down, except for the very, very rich, but they seemed inclined to marry on some yacht in the Caribbean or the Mediterranean, in a chateau in Switzerland or some island in the Pacific they rented for a week's celebration with two hundred of their closest friends. But there was something else he just couldn't put his finger on.

Randy turned away from his office window, from the weeping willow and walked back to his desk. He put his hand to his temples and rubbed and rubbed. He had a really, really bad headache. He looked at his silent phone. He straightened the large pad and pen that sat in the center of his neat desk. He looked around the antiqued filled room. He went over to the large wood easel that held a framed picture of the mansion that stated, "Have the wedding of your dreams at the Winthrop Manor." Although it didn't need straightening, he straightened it, anyway.

His back to the large, hand-carved wood double door, he didn't see Josie enter. She tipped-toed up to him and grabbed him around the waist, scaring the crap out of him. His face went white, as if he had seen a ghost.

"Josie! You scared the bejeezes out of me! What're you doing?"

"Being playful!" And then with a hint of seduction in her voice, "C'mon, Randolph Four, don't you like it when I'm playful?"

He straightened his tie and gave her a peck on the cheek.

"I'm sorry, Honey, but it's not a good day, at all."

She put her arms around his waist to comfort him, but he would have none of it.

"O-kay." She tried not to take it personally. "So what happened.?"

Anger rose in Randy's voice. "Nothing! Nothing happened. I thought this nice couple was going to book the place for their wedding. I was so sure of it. I'm telling you Josie, everything was going so great. Then while I was in here, drawing up the contract, they went and looked at the Grand Ballroom, again. They came back looking like someone spooked them or something. They hardly said good-by and ran out."

"That's weird," was all Josie could come up with.

"Why doesn't anyone want to get married, here? I just don't get it." Randy was beyond depressed as he went to his desk chair and plopped down.

Josie started rubbing his temples.

"Well, maybe they decided the Grand Ballroom was too big. Or, too... grand. You know, that could be it, Randolph Four," she said sympathetically.

"Stop making excuses, trying to make me feel better, Jos. I've only booked two weddings this whole year and a couple of cheap kid's parties. And how many times have I told you not to call me *that!* I hate it!

"Okay, Randy, calm down. Please."

Swiveling his chair around towards her, he looked like he almost had tears in his eyes.

"I'm sorry, Jos. Forgive me. It's just that I'm tapped out. I've used almost all my inheritance on this place. I owe the bank my life. If he were alive, my step-dad would probably call me such a stupid boy for the way I've wasted everything he left me. From what I know about them, it's like my Winthrop family all over again. I inherited... stupid"

"Stop that, Randy! Your grandfather was a gambler and had some really bad ah… business partners. You're not like any of them."

"And I didn't take a gamble fixing this old dump up?"

Josie tried to lighten the mood, but failed. "Well, at least you're not a druggie like your dad was."

Randy almost laughed. "Yeah, that makes me feel much better."

Josie looked at the photo of the Manor on the easel. "Hey, I've got a great idea! Why don't *we* get married here. I could get it into magazines and papers. It would be a great publicity ploy. 'Get married at the great Winthrop Manor and see how beautiful your day will be from a couple who knows, first hand…' And we'd take all these photos in the rose garden, in the Ballroom, even in the master bedroom! Whatta ya think?" She was excited.

Randy said nothing.

"Randy? What? We shouldn't get married here or we maybe shouldn't get married at all?"

"Neither," he said softly. "I mean, I can't Jos. Not right now."

She nodded her head, sadly and looked down at her engagement ring.

"You can't or you won't?"

"C'mon, Jos, we've been through this. I just can't get married with all this debt hanging over my head. I've got to figure out a way to get this place paid off, first, to be a success."

"That's what you've been saying since we got engaged. It's been years. Anyway, I don't care. It will pay off, I just feel it and in the meantime, I have a good job."

"I just can't, right now..."

She looked at him, tears now rolling down her cheeks. She wasn't going to beg, that's for sure. And so she just turned on her heel and started for the door.

"Josie, wait!. I love you... I do..."

But she was gone.

Not knowing what to do, his entire life seemingly falling apart before his very eyes, Randy went back to the window to see Josie running across the great, green lawn, passed the weeping willow toward the parking area.

Softly and sadly he said, "I love you, Josie... I do..."

CHAPTER FIVE

JOSH AND KATIE

Josh and Katie. Katie and Josh. Theirs was a match made in heaven, heaven being one of those numerous internet Matchmaking sites that had become so popular. Why, one might wonder, would two intelligent, good-looking, gregarious, in shape, single professionals such as they, feel the need to turn to the internet to meet anyone, much less a life partner? Well, the truth was, finding love in the new century was just much harder than it had been fifty, forty, thirty, even twenty years earlier. Relationships no longer seemed to be based on meeting and having real communication, but rather conversing on one's computer. Women were more prevalent in the work force and weren't sitting home waiting for prince charming to ride up on a white horse, sweep them away at a gallop, lock them in a mortgaged-to-the-hilt house where they would spend the rest of their life birthing babies, cleaning and cooking.

Katie Combs wanted to do something wonderful in her life. She was a nurturer, the person all her friends came to, to help them out with their problems. Coming from a close-knit family, she was a high school cheerleader, top of her class in school, on the tennis team and was just your well-scrubbed, all American girl. In high school, when all her friends were having those typical teen-age angst-filled days and nights, Katie would have what she called, 'Healing The Hysteria' evenings on Saturday nights in her bedroom. Katie never knew where it came from, but she just seemed to be born with the magic touch of being a great listener, then gently suggesting ways her friends might feel better, be it concerning their problems with their parents or with a boyfriend who had gone astray. She was all about helping them have self-worth and feeling good about their face, their bodies and their brains.

Although she was popular in high school and did have a semi-serious boyfriend in her senior year, she broke it off when he wanted her to travel around the globe with him for a year after graduation.

"I can't Michael, I want to go to college and become a therapist. I want to spend my life helping people with their problems."

"How 'bout my problem, Katie? Help me with my problem, which is you not wanting to go and see the world with me! You can get serious about your life, later!" Michael didn't get it.

Katie couldn't help him, instead enrolling at USC and four years later graduating at the top of her class. She then got her Masters in psychology, eventually becoming a Marriage and Family counselor. Her work was her life and it was only every now and again that she wondered if she was missing something, as she bought yet another bridesmaid dress, then attended baby shower after baby shower as her girlfriends went on their journey so different from the path she had taken.. It wasn't that men weren't interested in Katie and that she didn't date, it was the simple fact that as enlightened as men had become concerning women and what they desired in life, down deep, they still wanted and needed a home cooked meal, a clean house and a happy wife and children to come home to. Thirty years had passed since women had burned their bras for equality, to be respected for more than being a baby-machine, but Katie noted that in reality, not that much had changed, at all.

Josh Peterson grew up wanting to help people, too. His father had died in a car accident when he was not yet a teen. His mother went back to work out of necessity and now being the 'little man' of the house, Josh cared and cared well for his younger sister and brother. He, too, was popular, a football player in high school and an 'A' student. He, too, dated and truthfully, was the 'catch' for all the girls to fish for, but Josh, being a serious fellow had a one-track mind. He would go to a good college and work his fingers to the bone, any way he could, to help out his mother and siblings.

Living up the coast from Los Angeles, he got a football scholarship to the University of California at Santa Barbara. At first he had the dreams and the talent of becoming a professional football player, until a bad shoulder injury put that dream to rest, forever. While talking with his college counselor, one day, depressed as hell about his aborted future as a pro athlete, the counselor noticed what a sensitive and intelligent young fellow Josh Peterson was. He suggested Josh, perhaps, take some psyche classes and see where it might lead him. Three years later, it led him to decide to become a therapist. And that's exactly what he did become.

Eventually, he moved down to Santa Monica and started working in a clinic. And life was good and fulfilling for Josh. The only thing his life lacked was love, but he was working so hard and was so serious about his work, days, then months, then years passed and he hardly noticed. Hardly.

And then one fateful day, one of his colleagues said to him, "Josh, you're what, thirty, thirty-one? You're good looking and smart and a terrific therapist, but aren't you lonely, man?"

"I don't think about it that much," was Josh's answer.

"Bull crap!" said his colleague. "You can still work hard and find love. Here." And he handed Josh a card that stated, "*Matchmaker, Find Me A Match.* For the person who hates the idea of online dating." Of course, it was an on-line dating service.

Feeling it would be rude to decline or hand it back, Josh stuffed it in his pant's pocket, thanked his colleague and told him he'd think about it.

It hadn't been a week before, that a colleague of Katie's had handed her the same card, giving her the same speech. Katie hoped her colleague hadn't seen her roll her eyes as she smiled, sweetly, thanked her and put the card in her purse.

"You're not getting any younger, Katie. You're almost thirty. Don't you want to find eternal love?"

Katie laughed. "After the couples I see in my practice, I'm not sure there is such a thing,"

"Oh, just try it! What's the worst thing that could happen?" was her friend and colleague's answer.

I could be cyber lied to and meet a psycho crazy, or worse, a Republican, Katie thought.

Neither of them knew exactly what drove them to go on that dating site, perhaps momentary insanity, but they both did. Answering question after question whipped both Josh and Katie into a cold sweat.

"Describe the type of person you'd be interested in meeting."
She answered: Funny, goofy, funny, liberal, creative, funny, really intelligent, liberal, kind, funny.

"Name the personal habits of others that irritate you."
He answered: Not nice people. Not smart people. Desperate people. Proselytizing people. Right-wing conservative people. Phony people.

"Give a detailed description of yourself."
She answered: I think I think silly.
He answered: I think silly thoughts, but no one knows it.

"Your perfect date would be...?"

He answered: Ah, jeez, I don't know. I can't believe I'm doing this in the first place."

She answered: Ah, well, let's see... how about a long walk, barefoot on a sandy, white beach at sunset... in slow motion."

One might believe what happened next to be kismet.

Yes, they both put their toes into the cold water of cyber dating, but never actually had the guts to meet in the flesh, the folks behind 'profile' names such as, "LA HOT CHICK," or "LA DREAMER," or "LOVE BUNNY," or "SUPER DUDE."

And then one night, when both their 'free' month was about to expire, they gazed upon each other's profile and laughed. And the rest, as they say, is history. After cyber talking back and forth, then a number of real life phone calls, Josh and Katie timidly made a date to meet for coffee and realized they both hated coffee. And that was the start of something beautiful. Eight months later they moved in together and one year after their anniversary of matching up, Josh asked Katie to marry him. As a joke, later that day, she sent him an email accepting his proposal.

"I love you, I love you, I love you, Katie Combs!" he gushed.

Josh and Katie were sitting on the grass in a small local park enjoying a between appointments picnic lunch.

"And I love you, Joshua Peterson! Mm... Katie Peterson. I like it!"

Not caring who was watching, they kissed passionately. Then Katie looked at her beautiful, but not too large engagement ring and smiled.

"So, what should we do first?"

"First?"

"Oh, you men. For our wedding! We have to pick a date, register, find the perfect place, get a dress..."

"For me?" Josh laughed.

"Josh!" she laughed and elbowed him lightly. "Oh, and I have to pick bridesmaids and you, groomsmen, flowers, uh, oh, the cake, the rings. What else?"

"There's more?"

Katie thought a moment. "Oh yeah, the band, who's going to marry us, uh, the caterers, where to register. Did I say that, already? This is so exciting!"

Josh starting laughing. "I have an idea. How about we just elope to Vegas!"

"Right. And maybe have an Elvis impersonator officiate?"

"C'mon, Katie, that might be fun."

"No! This is the biggest day of our lives, at least, so far and I want it to be perfect."

"You're perfect." And he kissed her, again.

"Ah, don't you always know the right thing to say."

"Yes, I do!"

Katie looked at her watch. "Oh, crap, I have to get back to work. I have a patient at two."

"The agoraphobic or the schizophrenic?"

"Very funny, Josh. No, a very sweet, older man who's going through a divorce. His wife left him for a younger guy and I can't tell you anymore."

They ended their picnic and started walking, hand in hand.

"You?"

"A couple having problems with their teenager. And I can't tell you, anymore!" Josh laughed.

"I can't wait to have kids. You're going to make such a great daddy."

"And you a mommy!"

It was just all so sweet and wonderful between these two. They both felt they were destined to meet and be together until the end of time. But first they had to get through planning a wedding.

The first place they checked out for their nuptials was a private club over-looking the Pacific Ocean. A Mrs. Clara Layton gave them the grand tour. After seeing the large, fancy dining room, she led them out to the huge lawn where the wedding would take place. Although it was sunny out, it was October and a cold wind whipped around them.

"What we usually do," explained Mrs. Layton, "is have all the seats face the ocean. A string quartet could be placed over there. And Katie, you would emerge, a vision in white, down those stairs to a satin aisle strewn with rose petals, to meet your groom." Mrs. Layton, happy with herself and her sale's pitch smiled a phony smile.

"It's really beautiful here, isn't it Josh?" Katie said as she wrapped her sweater tighter around her.

"You'll never find a lovelier spot to be married in this town, believe me."

Josh walked out toward the bluff and breathed in the salt air. "To tell you the truth, Mrs. Layton, we're just a little concerned about the weather. You know, June gloom at the beach and all that."

Ever the saleswoman, Mrs. Layton explained. "No, no, no, no gloom. Especially toward the end of the month. When were you thinking of for your wedding date?"

Josh and Katie answered together. "The third."

"Oh... well, I must tell you that the last number of years there's been no gloom in June. Absolutely none! I think that's because that nasty El Nino never came to pass. No! No gloom! It'll be perfect! Warm and gloomless! Trust me!"

The next place Katie looked at was a fancy hotel in Santa Monica. This time her mother, Bonnie, was with her. Derek, the hotel wedding consultant gave them the tour of the grand ballroom. It was huge and empty.

"It's so big, Katie," said Bonnie.

Kidding, Katie said, "Well, maybe I'll just have to rent some people to fill the place up. Whatta you think about that idea, Mom?""

"You know", interjected Derek and ignoring anything humorous about the situation of renting the hall, "our hotel is a favorite with celebrities! Especially our Tiki Bar." Drinks could be served there after the ceremony and before dinner! Fabulous!"

Katie looked around the room, again. "Mom?"

Again, not waiting for an answer, Derek said, dramatically, "Just visualize, if you will, all the tables set around the dance floor, the band, the huge and luscious cake on a table in the corner, the flowers, the guests, all gussied up! To die for, no?"

Katie tried to visualize it and wondered if this was the place she wanted to have that first dance with her new husband.

"I don't know... Derek. It just doesn't have a lot of character, at least the kind I'm... visualizing."

"You want character!? I can do character! Anything you want! No problemo!"

"I'm sure you can and it's nothing personal, but I just don't think it's me, that's all." Katie and her mother started walking toward the ballroom's huge doors.

"Wait! I could make it you! Whatever theme you want. Hawaiian? American Princess? Casual chic? My Moonlight Sonata décor is to die for! Whatever you want!" Derek's desperation was showing.

Katie and her mother were almost out of the ballroom, but he wasn't giving up, following after them like a puppy dog needing attention.

"We're already getting booked for June so..."

But the women were out the door.

Derek stomped his foot on the floor. "Oh, drat!"

Katie and Josh spent the better part of the next few months looking for their perfect Shangri-La of a place to marry. And they were having no luck, what-so-ever.

"Maybe we should just elope to Vegas, after all" admitted a forlorn Katie.

"No, Honey, you have your heart set on the perfect place to get married and we're going to find it, I swear. I know how important this is to you."

"I don't know, Josh. It's not like I need anything really elaborate. It's just, sort of, I just think I'll know it in my bones when I see it, you know?"

"I know, Sweetie and we're going to find it."

He took her in his arms and tried to melt away her anguish with a kiss.

"Maybe I'm asking too much. Maybe my dream wedding place doesn't exist. Anyway, what's important is that we love each other and we're getting married and we're going to live happily ever after, right?"

"Right. And no matter how you look when you get up in the morning, you'll always be my Cinderella."

"Charming... Oh, hell, maybe we should just get married in my folk's backyard and save our money for a honeymoon in Hawaii, instead."

"Whatever you want, Baby. Whatever you want." And Josh meant it.

CHAPTER SIX

THE GHOSTS MATERIALIZE

Randy, always the salesman, was showing the Grand Ballroom at the Winthrop Manor to yet another perspective wedding couple, Ann and Nick. This was a second marriage for both of them. No longer spring chickens, as it were, they were both inching closer toward that fifty year old mark.

"This room holds up to three hundred people, but we have wonderful smaller rooms, also."

Ann gazed at the long, beautifully handcrafted wood bar, then to the huge windows that looked out to the meticulously kept Rose

Garden. "Your place is just so gorgeous, Mr. Winthrop."

"Please, call me Randy."

"Randy," she complied. "So this place is really a hundred years old? It almost looks like it was just built."

"Well, I spent years renovating it," Randy said proudly, "so it would look exactly like it did when my great-grandfather built it for my great grandmother. They were married, right here, in this very room. It was his wedding present to her."

"Romantic, huh, Ann?"

Ann couldn't tell if her soon-to-be second husband was being sarcastic or not. Was that annoyance that crossed her face?

"Are you going to build me a mansion, Nick?"

Nick lightly laughed. "Sorry, Honey, but I already built one for my ex wife. One mansion, one wife."

It didn't take a genius to feel the sudden tension between the two, as Ann turned away and walked around the room.

"Well, why don't I just let you folks look around and talk between yourselves. I'll be in my office, when you're ready."

When Randy walked out of the ballroom, Ann turned back to her 'soon-to-be' and gave him a very dirty look.

"What? What? I was just kidding, Ann."

"No, you weren't. And she's going to continue to take you for everything you're worth, isn't she? And you're going to give her every little thing she wants, because you feel so guilty for leaving her."

"Enough, Annie. And that's not true. Anyway, we don't need a big old mansion to live in, do we?"

Ann ignored him and went over to the long bar and ran her hand across the smooth wood. Suddenly, for no apparent reason, she yelled out and pulled her hand away, looking very frightened.

"What's wrong?" I said I was kidding." Nick went over to her and tried to make nice.

"I… I… I just… felt… something."

"Huh? Whatta ya mean, you felt something?"

Ignoring him, she put her hand back on the bar and again reacted, as if someone had slapped her hand, again, only this time harder.

"Ow!!!

"What is the matter with you?"

"Someone or something just put their hand on mine, then slapped it and tried to push it away. Twice!"

"That's ridiculous. Must have been your imagination."

Ann looked at him hard. "Why do you always do that, dismiss things I say you? I'm telling you that there's something on this bar that just slapped me!"

"I don't dismiss what you say, Dear, it's just sometimes you say, well, strange things."

"Really?! Well, why don't you put your hand on the bar and see what happens."

Nick rolled his eyes, then put his hand on the bar. Nothing. He moved his hand all over it and still nothing.

"See, Honey, nothing there."

"Don't 'Honey' me! I know what I felt."

Pissed, she started walking away from him. Still somewhat freaked, she looked all around the room, her eyes eventually looking up to one of the huge crystal chandeliers hanging from the ceiling. Just then, it started to sway back and forth, back and forth. Now Ann was really freaked.

"Nick… that chandelier, it's moving back and forth."

Nick looked up to see the swaying. "It's nothing. Probably just a small shaker."

"See! You're doing it again! Ya know, sometimes I really hate you!"

Suddenly the chandelier swayed back and forth, harder and harder.

"I'm getting out of here!" Ann was almost hysterical, now. "Something's weird about this place and it's not an earthquake. We're not moving. Nothing else is moving. The chandelier is moving!"

"Okay, I see it, I see it." Nick kept staring at it, almost as if he was being hypnotized by it. Back and forth, back and forth.

Not bothering to answer him, Ann ran out of the room. Nick suddenly, 'came to,' and hightailed it out the door, also.

With the couple gone, the chandelier suddenly stopped swaying. A moment later, a white, foggy ameba-shaped form floated down from the ceiling. As it reached the floor the white fogginess started to dissipate and the form of... Susanna began to appear, looking exactly the way she looked in 1928, close to eighty years earlier, when she was shot dead by Benny The Blimp, in that very room. She smoothed out her straight skirt and adjusted the beret on her head.

"Damn! I didn't even get a chance to really get started with them. Jack?! Jack? Where the hell are you?"

Another white foggy form materialized next to her. It was Jack, looking as dapper as he had that night, his gun still holstered around his shoulder.

"Where were you, Jack? I'm the 'bar' and you're the 'chandelier'! Do I have to do everything myself, for crying out loud?" She gave him a dirty look that could kill.

"Sorry."

"Yeah, Jack, you're always sorry, aren't you?" And she started to de-materialize back into her white foggy, ghostly self.

"Yeah, Susanna, just float away, like you always do. This isn't about now and you know it! How many times do I have to say I'm sorry? Huh? Huh?"

But she was gone, leaving Jack talking to thin air.

In his office, nervously waiting for Ann and Nick to return, wondering if he'd finally booked a wedding, Randy turned toward his window just in time to see the perspective newlyweds run across the great lawn toward their car. As they did, Nick tripped and almost fell to the ground.

"What the heck?" Randy said, under his breath. Then he started rubbing and rubbing his temples.

A week later, Randy was showing a young couple in their twenties, Carolyn and Freddie, the master bedroom of the Manor. He proudly pointed out the beautiful Tiffany lamps on the bed stands, the marble fireplace, the large Chinese throw rugs,

"Wow, this room is amazing, isn't it, Freddie?"

Freddie was not that impressed. "Pretty fancy, schmancy, don't you think, Carolyn? You really like all this old stuff?"

"Yeah! I do!" And she gave him a look that Randy couldn't help noticing.

"Whatever." said Freddie.

"This was actually my great-grandfather's bedroom. He bought all these antiques, some from Europe, everything in here, for my great-grandmother at the turn of the century. Theirs was a real love affair."

Carolyn sighed. "Oh, how romantic. Isn't that romantic, Freddie?"

Freddie continued to show a great lack of interest. "Yeah. Romantic."

"Well, I love it."

"It's your day, Baby," Freddie said as he patted her ass.

She elbowed him, hard. "Yours, too, dummy."

Embarrassed, but continuing to try to sell like a used car salesman, Randy continued. "Now, I don't know your honeymoon plans, but you can add to your wedding package, for not too much more money, and stay in this very room your first night together." There was just a tad of desperation in his smile.

"We live together, man." Freddie looked at Randy as if he were crazy.

"Yes, yes, of course, but what I meant was your, uh, first night together as husband and wife."

By this time one could cut the tension with a knife and so Randy left the couple alone to, hopefully, come to some conclusion in his favor.

"Jeez, Freddie, why are you being like that?"

"What? Like what?"

"You were rude to Mr. Winthrop, to begin with. And why don't you like this place? I love it."

"I don't know, Car, it reminds me of some old creepy movie. But if you like it, whatever."

"But I want you to like it," she almost whined.

"I like it, I like it. Okay?"

Carolyn shook her head and walked over to the huge canopied bed, feeling the soft, thick comforter, with both her hands. She then gingerly laid down on it, posing herself in what she considered to be a seductive pose.

"C'mon, Honey," she purred. "Wouldn't you just love to do it on this bed. Ooh, it's so soft and comfy."

Freddie laughed and joined her on the bed. "You mean right now, Baby? Huh? Huh? You wanna do it right now? Right here?"

She started to giggle as he plunked himself down on top of her.

"Well, maybe just a little make-out...." She continued in a breathy voice.

And they started, to put it mildly, make-out.

Then Carolyn suddenly started to scream. "Oh my God, oh my God, oh my God!!" and pushed Freddie off her, scrambling off the bed onto the floor, taking him with her.

"What the hell is the matter with you, girl?"

Scared out of her mind, she breathed heavily. "Someone... someone... or something... goosed me, good!"

"What? You're crazy, Carolyn!"

By now she was quite hysterical. "I'm telling you, Freddie, I know a goose when I get a goose and I got goosed!"

Freddie looked hard at her, then crept back up on the bed, patting it all over with his hands.

"You're nuts! There's nothing here."

"I wanna get outta here. I wanna go home," she cried as she started crawling on hands and knees toward the bedroom door.

Just then, as Freddie continued patting the bed, a pillow hit him hard on the head, not once, but twice! Stunned, he started screaming, "Run, Honey, run for your life!"

Freddie tumbled off the bed and started dragging Carolyn up on her feet and out of the room. In the long hallway, outside the bedroom, they almost smashed into Randy, who had come back to check to see if they had made a decision, yet.

Guess not. In disbelief, he watched them run away, still screaming. He then peered, apprehensively, into the master bedroom, saw that everything was quiet and neat and walked out, again, shaking his head.

In the middle of the giant, canopied bed, a white and foggy image appeared, slowly materializing into, you guessed it, Randolph Winthrop The First, wearing the striped pajamas he took his last, living breath in.

"Millie? Millie, are you there? Where are you? Where are you, my Millie?"

Another white foggy image slowly emerged on the large chair, across from the bed, the very chair that Mildred had died sitting on. Soon, she also materialized, looking like the sweet old woman she was forty years before, on the day of her death.

"Millie, my Darling, you were supposed to slam the window, remember? Why didn't you slam the window like you always do? Did you forget, my Honey Bunny?"

"No, Randolph One, I didn't forget! I didn't feel like it! And I'm not your Honey Bunny! But you sure seemed to be having fun with that girlie, weren't you? You're a dirty old, lecherous man, that's what you are!" Her frail voice was beyond hostile.

"Hey! No one sleeps on this bed except me and you, Millie. No one does kissy-kissy face, here! It's our wedding bed!"

"Are you out of your mind, old man? It'll be a cold day in the underworld before I sleep in that bed, again… or kissy anything with you!"

"Oh, for goodness sake, Mildred, a hundred years, it's been a hundred years."

"It hasn't been a hundred years! That's why you went broke, among other stupidities. You had no head for numbers. And yet, I continued in that bed with you for over fifty years! Fifty years, not a hundred!"

"The best years of my life, my Mildred. And then you went and broke my heart. Yes, you did," he said, sadly.

"You broke my heart, first, you cheater!"

"Aren't you ever going to forgive me for my one little transgression, Millie?"

"No!"

And then she disappeared into a filmy fog.

"But I love you, my Mildred. You've always been the girl for me. I love you."

There was no response from his wife, so Randolph The First just stared, sadly, at the chair that was now empty, except for the last hazy white remains of Mildred. Then he slowly disappeared, too.

In his office a few weeks later, Randy was rubbing and rubbing his temples, as he looked out toward the weeping willow. He had just shown the Manor to, yet another bride and groom-to-be, Vanessa and Ty, but even he had to admit they didn't look like the kind of couple who would appreciate saying their vows at the sophisticated setting he had to offer. He watched, through his window, as the two sat on the lawn and talked. Ah, to be a fly on the great tree.

Both Vanessa and Ty were decked out in black leather pants, jackets and boots. In the parking area sat Ty's huge and shiny motorcycle.

Vanessa always had this inner inkling that he possibly loved that cycle more than he loved her.

"Ya know, Vanessa, I really don't think our friends will be comfortable at a place like this," Ty said as he popped a cigarette out of his jacket pocket and stuck it in his mouth.

"Our wedding isn't for them! It's for me! And you. I like it here, Ty. It's so pretty and peaceful." She looked up at the willow, its leaves blowing softly in the breeze.

"Yeah, well maybe out here, but that ballroom? Give me a break! We're not hoity-toity like that."

Now Vanessa was getting angry. "It could be me! I have class! If it were up to you we'd be married in the parking lot of Ernie's Tattoo Parlor and it'd be catered by Taco Bell!"

"Hey, that sounds like a great idea!"

She punched him in the arm, hard!

"Oww!!! That hurt! You're an evil chick, you know that?"

Vanessa laughed, "And that's the way you like me, isn't it?"

"Damn straight! But ya know what I think? I think you want to go all fancy to impress your step-mother, with all her richie-rich friends, that's what I think!"

Vanessa's mood changed faster than a speeding train. "You're a jerk, Ty. Sometimes I wonder why I even want to marry you in the first place." And she socked him, again, this time in the other arm."

"Oww! Will you stop it?!"

Pissed, Ty got up and started to walk around the tree in a huff. Suddenly and for no good reason, whatsoever, he tripped and fell to the ground.

Vanessa couldn't help but laugh. "You are such a clumsy boob! Okay, ya know what, forget the ballroom, we could have the ceremony and the reception right out here, under this tree."

Ty picked himself up and made sure his leather pants hadn't been damaged in the fall.

"Good one, Vanessa. This is a weeping willow tree. Bad omen, I say."

"Ya know what, nothing ever satisfies you!" Now Vanessa was pissed, again

Although there was only that slight breeze, a good-sized branch suddenly fell out of the tree, almost hitting Vanessa.

"Holy crap!" Vanessa quickly got up and ran to Ty, hugging him.

"See, it is an omen. There's something weird about this place. I just feel it in my gut. Let's get outta here!"

"It just caught me by surprise. It was just a branch. Branches fall out of trees all the time. I think the truth is, you just don't want to marry me, not here, not anywhere."

"You know what the truth is? I'll tell you the truth. The truth is you're one crazy broad! Now, let's split!"

Just then, Ty's prized cycle fell over with a crash.

"What the hell…? My wheels! We're getting' outta here, now!" Ty yelled, as he dragged Vanessa toward the parking area. He righted his cycle, checked it for any damaged, revved the engine loudly and took off, with Vanessa holding onto to him for dear life.

Randy walked out of the front door of his Manor, just in time to see the dust rise in the parking area. Totally, depressed, he walked back inside, wishing he had something stronger to take than aspirin for his throbbing head.

At the weeping willow a white fogginess materialized into the lovely Heather, flowers still in her long and flowing hair. A moment later another white fogginess floated near to her and emerged as Jimmy.

"What a bitchin' hog!"

Heather spoke slowly and deliberately to him. "Do not speak to me of hogs. Do not speak to me of anything, Jimmy."

"You don't have to talk so slowly, Heather. I'm not stoned, anymore."

With even more hostility she said, "Do not speak to me about getting stoned, getting on your hog, hitting this weeping willow and KILLING me!"

"Yeah, well, I died, too." Then in his best Brando impersonation, he went on, "Ya know, I coulda been a contenda." And then he lightly laughed.

But Heather was having none of it. "Good for you. I could have made a difference in the world!"

"Oh, so you think that's why the world has gone nuts? 'Cause you weren't around to make it better?" he said with a sarcastic tone.

"Shut up, Jimmy!" And in a flash, she was gone.

Jimmy, possibly regretting his words, shook his head, then slowly disappeared into the breeze.

CHAPTER SEVEN

LIFE AND DEATH AND PURGATORY

Life: "The opposite of... dead." "The ability to function." "The period for which a person or organism is or has been or will be... alive." Yes, there are many, many definitions of "life." On the other hand, some folks are dead, inside, while they're alive. Life is what we know to be living upon this earth at a particular time. But why are we born? Why do we inhabit certain bodies for a certain duration? Why do the good die young? Why, why, why?

Death: "The opposite of... life." "The end of life as we know it." "Cessation of all vital functions." "The end or destruction of something." Yes, there are many, many definitions of death. But what happens to us when we die? Oh, there are lots of answers to that question, depending on who you ask. Some think we go to heaven. Some think we go to hell. Some think there is... nothing. Blackness. Nothing... forever and ever. Nothing.

Heaven: "A place of complete bliss, delight and peace." "The abode of God and of the righteous after death." Yes, yes, there is more than one definition of Heaven. But some say they have found Heaven on Earth. Good for them, I say.

Hell: "A place of suffering, pain and turmoil in the afterlife." "The nether world in which the dead continue to exist." "The realm of the devil." "Demons in which the damned suffer everlasting punishment." And yes, there are more than a few definitions of Hell. On the other hand, some people are always complaining that their life is... hell. And so, is hell here... or there? Or everywhere?

Reincarnation: "To bring back a soul after death." "Coming back in another body, in which the soul lives on." And if one believes this, we keep coming back and coming back and coming back until we have learned our lessons, all our lessons and we reach the ultimate... Nirvana! Why, one must wonder, can't we get it right the first, maybe the second time around? You know, sort of a, "cut to the chase" thing. And once we hit Nirvana, then what? Where do we go? Heaven? Who the hell knows!

Purgatory: "A temporary condition of torment or suffering." "A state in which the souls of those who have died in a state of grace must expiate their sins." "A way station on the path to heaven." "A condition or process of purification or temporary punishment in which souls who die are made ready for Heaven." "Where a person undergoes judgment in which the soul's eternal destiny is specified." Wow! There are a lot of definitions of Purgatory.

And so, is it within one's belief system, as to what Life, Death, Heaven, Hell and Purgatory really are? Or is there one true truth to what the hell we are doing before, during and after birth, as we know it? Only problem is, we don't know it. We just hope, believe, pray and on and on that what we believe is true. Otherwise, our life can be hell or we live in a state of purgatory while on this earth.

Our six ghosts once lived. And then they died. The question, among many, is where are they and what the hell are they doing there, will they stay there forever and a day, or what do they have to do to, shall we say, move on... and

then... to where? And you think Randolph
Winthrop The Fourth had a headache?

A short recap. Jack and Susanna were
married, then later killed in the Grand Ballroom
of the Winthrop Manor in 1928, by the bullets of
Benny The Blimp. Bummer. Oh, they both had
big dreams of doing wonderful things in their
lives, lives that were cut short, much to early.
Suzanna wanted to change the world with her
activism. Jack wanted to be a great writer, to
inspire the masses with his written word. Her
causes went on without her and his words were
never read. And so, for some reason, the once
lovebirds, floated around the Manor, alone, for
over thirty years. It must be said, though, that not
a day went by that Jack didn't try his hardest to
get back into Susanna's good graces. But she
was having none of that. A bitter ghost she was.
And then, one day, Randolph One
appeared, more or less. He immediately
recognized Jack, after all, they had been in
business together. But with age and wrinkles,
Jack couldn't believe this old man who had
materialized, before his eyes was, in fact, the
namesake of the great Manor.
Once the shock diminished, first that Jack
and Susanna were not longer alone and second,
that it was Randolph One who had joined them,

they got to reminiscing about the good old days, which Susanna didn't think were all that good. When 'the wife' was out floating around, Jack and Randolph quietly talked about Benny The Blimp and even how that party was going to be Jack's last one, that he was going to, as he put it, take all the money and run, not give Randolph his cut and finally have a bootlegging-free life with his love, Susanna. Learning that, Randolph, luckily, didn't hold a grudge. He didn't have to, since after the bullets stopped flying that night, Randolph got the night's take, knowing where Jack had it hidden it. A short time after that, Randolph One stiffed Benny The Blimp, royally, since he was the one who got the fat gangster put away for life.

But besides the camaraderie between the two, the old man was sad and broke into tears at a moment's notice. That is, until his beloved, Mildred showed up on the scene, a few years later. From that moment on, he spent all his time trying to woo back his wife, the love of his life. No luck. A bitter ghost was she, also.

Then, in the early 1970's, the young hippy couple, Heather and Jimmy, joined them. It was almost as if they were Susanna and Jack reincarnated... but they weren't. At the great weeping willow tree where they had been married, Heather and Jimmy died, a top his hog.

She had wanted to change the world, also, through politics. He, through his songs of peace and freedom. But neither was to be.

Imagine the two young couple's surprise, one balmy spring day, when they first materialized in front of each other. Yes, surprise, wonderment, depression, anger, every emotion possible, went through these four souls. The women found a real simpatico with each other and spent hours upon hours talking about the world they had lived in and world they left. Since she and Mildred never spoke of such things, it was hard for Susanna to imagine it had taken all those years for women to finally stand up and demand their rights. She had thought that might have happened by the 1940's. My goodness, at least by the 1950's. But she got a huge kick from learning that women were burning their bras to make their point. And it was gratifying that she, they, women could finally be and do anything they desired, that they didn't need a man to make them happy. Oh, how she longed to get her hands on some copies of that newly published Ms Magazine, Heather told her about.

Jack and Jimmy had their creativity in common. And while Jack dabbled in bootlegged liquor, Jimmy did the same with dope. Jack regaled Jimmy with all his wonderful story ideas, pissed that he would never have that best selling novel, while Jimmy sang Jack his songs of change and peace and sit-in's and war protests. That didn't really interest Jack as much as learning that liquor was finally legal and mused how had he lived, he would have opened the swankest saloon, made such a good living at it, he could spend his days hunched over his Smith-Corona, his vast imagination typed onto pages, waiting for publication. Jimmy, of course dreamed of being bigger than the Beatles, traveling the world with his band and winning multiple Grammy's for his songs.

Whatever was going on in the Manor for the living, had little to no consequence to the six who seemed destined to spend eternity in their purgatory of anger and down-right hostility, concerning their lives and especially each other. As the years rolled on and on, it was the men who were constantly trying to get back into their wives good graces, while it was the wives who just couldn't seem to let the past be the past, never letting go of their anger of how their individual lives had turned out. You see, when you're dead, you seem only to care about your own feelings, of what you wanted, of what you didn't have, of what could have been. Of course, it could be surmised, that could also apply to the living, couldn't it?

Years later, once the Manor had become a wedding site, the six ghosts decided to take other people's destinies into their own hands, white and filmy as they were. It also gave them something to do. Being dead, even in a nice place, didn't have that many options when it came to having a quest in... life.

And so they carefully watched as would-be-brides and grooms came onto the grounds, looking for the perfect location to start their own lives together. And they didn't like what they saw. It was obvious most of these folks shouldn't be married, at all, as far as they were concerned. They witnessed the hostility, the out and out fights, the non-communication between would-be husbands and wives. No, they wouldn't let what led they, themselves, down the not-so primrose path, happen to others. In their minds, they were doing them a service. And it was then they decided that those many, many folks who had picked mates poorly, as far as they were concerned, those who insisted on being wed, yes indeedy, the ghosts made sure as hell it wouldn't be at the great Winthrop Manor. No, not over their dead bodies.

To be honest, this was all the doing of the women, whom after all these years, still were angry at they way they had sometimes lived and died with their mates. The men, for their part, went along, hoping to make points with the women they needed forgiveness and love from.

And so it came to pass that Susanna slapped people's hands at the wood-crafted bar, while Jack swayed the chandeliers, while Randolph One goosed unsuspecting brides-to-be, while Mildred slammed the bedroom windows (when she felt like it), while Jimmy tripped people and while Heather dropped weeping willow branches on their heads. Having some fun, now.

The truth was, these ghost were, how could one put it... inept... that is, at being, well, really good ghosts. But one couldn't fault them, since while they lived, ghosts and the supernatural and subjects such as these, just wasn't something any of them were interested in. They never really made a study of what they might be able to do in the state they were in. Perhaps had they have died under more terrifying circumstances, like, perhaps, a grizzly murder in the forest where axes were involved, perhaps had they have been really, really bad folks while alive, a serial killer, a Hitler... perhaps had they, at least, have read any ghostly literature, then maybe, maybe they could have been more professional as ghosts. As it were, they were just a bit more menacing than Casper.

Meeting in the dirty underbelly of the Manor were the fully materialized ghosts. Sitting on the large furnace were Jimmy and Jack. On chairs, were Randolph One and Mildred and on a table, legs dangling, were Susanna and Heather.

"I think we did quite well today, don't you, my Millie?" asked Randolph.

"Oh, yes, Randolph One, you got your daily dose of goosing in, didn't you? Aren't you proud of yourself? And stop calling me "My Millie. I haven't been yours in, in… twenty-five years." Hostility seethed out of her old mouth.

"Oh, my Millie… Millie, how many times do I have to tell you, no one, no one even sits on our love bed! And I certainly could not have hit a lady over the head with a pillow. I'm a gentleman, for goodness sake," he said with all innocence.

Mildred could only give her once husband the evil eye.

"Winthrop's! Winthrop's!! Let's not fight. We're all just trying to do our jobs. All except you, Jack." This from Susanna. "Again, I had to sway the chandeliers! What were you doing? Were you even there?"

"I'm bored, Susanna," complained Jack. "Jeez, I wish I had a typewriter. I could finish my novel."

"Oh, Jack, give it up, already," said Susanna. "And what would you call it? 'Notes From A Dead Man?' 'I Once Was Lost, But Now I'm... Dead?'

"Good one, Susanna," laughed Heather. "Anyway, Jack, typewriters are passé, One writes on these things called computers, now," said Heather.

"What's a computer?" asked Jack.

"They're these, I don't know, complicated machines that do, well, everything..." started Heather, only to be interrupted by Jimmy.

"Ignore her, Jack. She's been snooping around Randolph The Fourth's office, again"

"Hey, somebody has to know what's going on in this world." Heather came back with.

"Ah, my great-grandson. Randolph Winthrop The Fourth. What a boob," put in Randolph One. "He's not worth thinking about."

"Don't call our only living family member a boob!" This, of course from Mildred. "And what do you know? You spend your days and nights in that bed..."

"... Waiting for your return, my Dear. Waiting for your return."

"Yes, well, it will be, pardon the expression, a cold day in... Hades, before that happens."

"Stop it! Stop it!," yelled Heather. "I can't take another minute of this... whatever this is." And she quickly dissolved.

"Wait, Heather! Wait for me..." And Susanna did the same.

"What's up with those chicks, anyway? Ya do and ya do and nothing satisfies them," complained Jimmy.

"Yeah, they bat their baby-blues, get you hooked around their little finger and then, zap..." Jack said, shaking his head.

"Men!" And Mildred followed in the other women's wake.

"Come back, Millie. Don't leave me..."

The three men looked at each other, all shook their heads and at the same time said, "Girls!"

CHAPTER EIGHT

JOSH AND KATIE FIND THE WINTHROP MANOR

Spring was almost ready to spring, although, truth be told, it had been such a mild winter in Southern California, the trees and the flowers were in a manic state, leaves falling from trees too late and flowers blooming too early. A couple of days of the heavens letting loose with rain and the inevitable happened. Mud slides, road closures, slick roads which caused numerous car accidents, because folks in Los Angeles, didn't do well when moisture hit the streets. Heck, most people didn't know how to turn on their windshield wipers, they were used so infrequently. But that beacon on the hill, the great Winthrop Manor was looking spiffy as Randolph Winthrop The Fourth held out hope that this would be the spring that would change his life for the better, one way or another.

Unfortunately, it wasn't going too well, as engaged couples continued to run out of the Manor, fear in their eyes, hearts beating a mile a minute, from being slapped, goosed, tripped and the like by the ghosts.

Randy and Josie hadn't been getting along, either, which only added to his headaches and her wondering if she was simply wasting her time with him. But love is a funny thing. It's so very hard to let go when a light still flickers in one's heart.

It was night at the Manor. After a dismal day of getting no bookings, not even a nibble, Randy, half asleep, was slumped over his desk in his office. He was one depressed puppy. He didn't hear Josie quietly enter. She tip-toed over to him and knelt down.

"Hey, you..."

"Josie!" Randy's heart woke up and beat quickly.

"I'm sorry, Randy. I don't want to fight with you, anymore."

"No, no, I'm sorry."

"No, it was all my fault. I've been insensitive and selfish. I do understand why you want this place to be a success before we get married."

"No, Josie, I'm the one who's been insensitive and selfish. You were right. We've been together so long and you've been so patient."

At that point, they looked into each other's eyes and kissed, just like in the movies.

"This is all crazy. But I've made a decision, Jos. This place has become an... octopus around my neck."

"Don't you mean an albatross?" she lightly laughed.

"No, really?"

"Yeah. An albatross. A burden."

"Ah, well, I said octopus, 'cause I feel like I'm getting strangled to death by this place."

"She thought a moment. "Oh, then maybe you meant a boa constrictor." And she laughed again.

"It's not funny, Jos. This place is killing me. I've come to a conclusion, though. There's only one thing to do. I'm selling it."

"What? You can't do that!"

"Why not? It's all fixed up again. Hopefully, I'll be able to make a bundle, pay off all my debts to the bank and finally be free of the whole darn thing."

"But Randy, it's your family home. It's your heritage. Your entire history is in these walls. Isn't there another way?"

Randy got up and started pacing the room.

"No! And history of what, Josie? Of divorce and greed and bankruptcy. Of illegal activities. Of death. It's not like it's been a hundred years of happy memories, ya know."

She met him in the middle of the room. "Are you really sure about this? I don't want you doing something you're going to regret."

"I'm sure. And I want to marry you, soon. And not here! We'll find a nice, small place to live and we'll have a bunch of kids and..."

She didn't let him say another word. She just kissed him again and again.

"I love you, Randolph Four.."

"I love you, too, The Future Mrs. Randolph Four. So, I have one more couple coming tomorrow, but I'm sure they won't book the place, then I'm not advertising anymore, I'm finding a good realtor and that's that!"

Josie looked deeply into his eyes, then hugged him tightly. But what she didn't see, or didn't want to see was the pure sadness in his eyes.

Josh and Katie still had not found the perfect venue for their nuptials and considering they wanted a June wedding, this was becoming problematic. Time was running short, since most weddings are planned months, sometimes years in advance. They had seen pretty much every hotel in the city and nothing was right, at least, as far as Katie was concerned. Too big. Too small. Too elegant. Too dumpy. Too expensive. And on and on. Maybe driving to Vegas and being married by an Elvis impersonator wasn't such a bad idea, after all, she thought, in a moment of total frustration.

And then her mother, Bonnie, told her of this place in the Hollywood Hills she had heard of from a friend, The Winthrop Manor. Katie looked the place up on the internet and it seemed quite nice, if not a tad extravagant, but she decided it was worth taking a look at.

Driving up the long, winding driveway to the Manor with Josh, Katie looked out the car window.

"Wow. This place is huge. And so beautiful. Who knew it was even here."

"Nice," said Josh.

"Yeah. I just hope it isn't true, though."

Josh pulled into the large parking area and stopped the car.

"What isn't true? Katie? What aren't you telling me?"

"Well, there might, I said, might... be just a little, itty-bitty problem with it."

"Uh oh. What kind of a problem?" he asked her.

"Well, see, when I was looking the place up on the internet, after my mom told me about it, there were some corresponding links to go on and..."

"...And what?"

"Well, ya know how people rate everything on the internet?"

"Yeah." Josh was getting a bad feeling.

"Okay, of course it's stupid, but some people mentioned that sort of strange things happened when they visited the place. Now, don't laugh and who can believe rumors, or the internet, for that matter, but some people think it's... haunted."

"Haunted? You mean, like ghosts, haunted?"

"Crazy, huh? C'mon. Let's see for ourselves." She got out of the car, followed by Josh and they started walking across the great lawn to the mansion.

"Ya know, I once took a course in the paranormal and more than a few people believe in ghosts." He then started waving his hands in her face, pretending to scare her. "I see dead people. Are you scared?" he laughed.

"Ooh, yeah. But, ya know, I read that if ghosts really do exist, there's a good reason they stay and haunt a place."

They were now at the front door and Katie rang the bell.

Kidding, Josh said, "Okay, now, let's be on the lookout for them, okay?"

"I'm on the case," laughed Katie.

As they waited to be let in, six white, filmy forms floated up behind them. Suddenly Josh and Katie turned around at the same time, but saw nothing. They both started to laugh, nervously.

Without much enthusiasm, Randy gave Katie and Josh the grand tour. In one of the long hallways, Katie and Josh were admiring the painting on the wall of the whole Winthrop gang. Floating behind them were the six filmy ghosts.

"This was painted right before my great-grandfather died. He was very old and sick, but it was important to him to have a painting done with his newest heir, which was me." How many time had Randy told this story?

"It's sad you never got to know him," said Katie.

"No, but I've heard stories…"

They continued walking down the hall, the six ghosts, right behind them.

"So, Randy, is it true this place is haunted? That there are ghosts around here?" asked Josh, innocently.

"Josh!" said a surprised Katie.

"Haunted? Of course not," answered Randy. "I moved back here seven years ago, after my father's death and believe me, if this place was haunted, if there were ghosts around, I'm sure I would have seen them." And he laughed, lightly, if not uncomfortably.

The ghosts got a kick out of this, waving their filmy arms around the three. One of the forms seemed to elbow another. It was Jack and Jimmy.

"But you must have heard the rumors," asked Katie.

"Oh, sure," answered a still very uncomfortable Randy. "But, ah, truthfully, there isn't an old house in this town that people don't say is haunted. You know, dead movies stars sticking around and stuff like that."

As it had turned out, the night before, when Randy and Josie had been talking, Heather had, again, floated into the office and heard Randy's declaration of selling the Manor. Down in the basement she had told her compatriots what she had heard.

"Selling my home! Unacceptable!" said an outraged Randolph One. "Millie, we have to do something!"

Mildred said nothing, rolling her eyes.

Jack put in his two cents worth. "Maybe if we stop scaring folks and let them get married, here, he won't sell."

"But then, what'll we do?" This from Jimmy. "It's the highlight of my day!"

"I say we do what we always do. If we think couples shouldn't marry, we continue scaring them. We're doing them a favor," said Susanna.

"Of course, Dear, they'll probably get married, anyway, somewhere else. We have no control over that, do we?" Mildred added, in her always motherly way.

Heather thought about the situation for a moment. "I say, we do what we do and let the chips fall where they may."

And so it was decided in a four to two vote. Randolph The First, voted against it, of course and Mildred abstained. Majority wins.

And so in the Grand Ballroom, Katie's hand got slapped, Jack swayed the chandeliers back and forth and in the master bedroom Mildred slammed the window open and closed and Randolph The First, lightly goosed Katie, but with less enthusiasm than usual.

Katie, Josh and Randy came out of the Manor's front door after the tour.

"I love it! I think it'll be perfect!" said an excited Katie.

Of course, this took Randy by total surprise. "You do? I mean, that's great!"

"Believe me, Katie and I have seen so many places and, truthfully, this is the first one that really... feels right," said Josh smiling.

"It does?" Randy couldn't believe what he was hearing.

"So, you're sure you have openings in June?"

"Oh, yes, Katie, I'm very sure."

Josh looked all around the grounds and said, "Tell you what, it looks like a go, but we'll call you in a day or so to finalize everything. Is that okay?"

"Okay? It's great. Great!" said a happy for the first time in months, Randy. "And don't you two worry about anything. I'll give you a wedding day you won't ever forget!"

"You know what I just thought. My aunt and uncle want to renew their vows on their 40th anniversary in the fall.. I'm going to have them call you," said Katie.

"Wow! Thanks," said a now even more excited Randy.

They all shook hands and then Randy watched Katie and Josh start their trek across the great lawn to where their car was parked. Had he have not walked back into the Manor, he would have seen Josh trip a few times on the lawn and a branch almost hit Katie on the head as she walked under the weeping willow.

The couple showed no reaction to any of this, as they quickly got into their car and sped off.

As soon as it took the six ghosts to float, pell-mell to the basement, a meeting was in session.

"I don't get it, I tripped that guy three times and he had no reaction, then before they got into their car, I added a little something. I breathed right down that chick's neck and she didn't even flinch!" said an exasperated Jimmy.

"It's the 21st Century, Jimmy, they're not called 'chicks' anymore!" This, of course, from Heather.

"Sorry. Ladies."

"Women! Women! We're women, Jimmy! In fact, we were always women!" screamed an angry Heather.

"Chicks, Sweeties, Gals, Babes... Women. They're all the same," laughed Jack.

Susanna had heard enough. "Shut up, Jack! Now, can we get back to this couple?"

"Katie and... Josh," interjected Mildred, softly.

Randolph One, already half forgetting about the possible sale of his home, looked lovingly at the love of his life. "You're still sharp as a tack, Millie." Getting her back, would always be his main priority.

She gave him a dirty look.

"Okay, okay! But the branch almost falling on her didn't even raise an eyebrow," said Heather. "That's just plain weird. Isn't it? That never happened before."

"It is. Randolph One, are you sure you did the goosing thing?" asked Susanna.

"Oh, he never misses that opportunity," said the hostile as always, when it came to that subject, Mildred.

"It's just my job, Darling. You know that," said Randolph One.

"Whatever..." spat back Mildred.

"Winthrop's, please! Enough, already," yelled Susanna. "Mildred, did you slam the window?"

"Yes, yes. I slammed."

"No reaction when I swayed the chandelier," added Jack.

"Hm. How 'bout that. And she didn't react when I slapped her hand at the bar and pushed it away, either," said Susanna. "Something creepy is going on."

"Think we're losing our touch, after all this time?" asked Heather.

"Might I just say something? Did it ever occur to any of you that maybe these two, this Katie and Josh, really *should* be married. Perhaps their love is so strong they only see each other and all else doesn't exist," explained Mildred.

"Beautifully stated, my love," said Randolph One.

The others just looked at her as if she were crazy.

That night in their bed, snuggled up together, Katie and Josh went through, yet again, the extraordinary day's events.

"So, really, Katie, you're absolutely sure?"

"I'm sure, Josh. My hand was pushed off the bar. First slapped, then pushed right off the bar."

"And your tushy got pinched?"

They both burst out laughing.

"I swear, that almost pushed me over the edge. My heart started beating a mile a minute."

"You're my brave Katie. And what was with me tripping on the lawn? If this was really a ghost, or two, they're not very good at what they do, huh?"

"Well, maybe they just died, recently and aren't very... I don't know, practiced at being ghosts."

The two started laughing, again, at the very idea of what they were even considering.

Josh then thought for a moment. "Although, maybe I did really trip on my own on the lawn. Maybe this whole thing is in our imagination. We hear the place is possibly haunted and we let our mind do tricks. We of all people should know that can happen. I mean, we've spent years studying the human psyche. It's what we do."

"You could be right, but what if there really are ghosts, I mean, there and what if they really get violent or something and our wedding gets ruined?"

"We don't have to get married, there, Katie. I'm sure we can find another place. This whole thing is just really, really weird, huh?"

"But I love that place. Something is just drawing me there, to be married there. There has to be a reason, don't you think, Josh?"

Trying to quell her reservations, Josh said, "Listen to us. We're talking about this place really being haunted, with... ghosts! Like I said, maybe we were just looking for something strange to happen and in our minds, it did."

Katie started laughing. "On my ass, it did!"

"Okay, I'm beat. Let's get some sleep and worry about it, tomorrow, okay?"

He closed his eyes and was asleep in seconds.

"You think there's something to worry, about? Josh?" Seeing he was dead to the world, Katie just lay curled up in the safety of his arms, her eyes remained opened wide.

CHAPTER NINE

THANK GOODNESS FOR THE GOOGLE

As Josh slept soundly though the night, hardly moving, (isn't that the way it always is with men?), Katie tossed and turned. Unable to sleep, she finally, quietly, padded her way into the kitchen and made herself some hot tea, but it didn't do the trick. She turned on the TV in the living room and tried to watch an old Tracy and Hepburn movie, Pat And Mike, but couldn't concentrate, even though it was one of her favorites. She tried going back to sleep, again, counting sheep, only it turned into counting ghosts.

Finally, when she knew sleep would not be forthcoming that night, she went to her computer and did what one does when they have a question that needs answering. She hit the Google button. 'Winthrop Manor.' 'History Of.' 'Deaths In.' Hours later, as the sun finally made an appearance, she had learned more than she had possibly wanted. And oh my, it was fascinating.

A Jack Danton and his wife, Susanna, had been married at and years later died at the Winthrop Manor, killed by a Benny The Blimp. A bootlegger and a Communist activist, in the late 1920's, a match made in heaven, she thought to herself. What could those two possibly have in common, she thought.

Another article was all about Randolph Winthrop The First who had built and married his wife at the Manor. The article implied the old man was getting kick-backs from Danton's bootlegging, but it was never proved. After making and losing several fortunes, his wife, Mildred left him. Adultery was hinted as the real reason. He died in his bed at the Manor in his 80's, broke and heartbroken having never won back his 'prized possession,' his wife. She moved back into the house and a few years later, died there, also. This was in 1960.

In the early 1970's, the Winthrop Manor hit the newspapers, yet again. At a hippy love-in on the Winthrop grounds, a stoned wanna-be songwriter and singer, Jimmy Callen, had crashed his motorcycle into a huge willow tree, with his wife, Heather McGuire, a Political Science major in college, hanging on to him for dear life. They too had been married at the Manor a year before. Married and died. Married and died. Married and died at the Winthrop Manor. Interesting.

Pictures of the couples accompanied the articles. The more Katie read and stared at the photos, the more intrigued was she. When Josh finally woke and before he had swallowed his first sip of strong, black tea, Katie began regaling him with what she had learned through the night.

"So, don't you find it interesting that all these three couples were married and died at the Winthrop Manor? Three couples, different decades, married and died there."

Josh had to laugh. "Maybe you're in the wrong field, Honey. Maybe you should have been a detective instead of a therapist!"

"Well, as therapists, aren't we sort of detectives, of the mind?" she answered back.

"Mm, I like that. Good one," he chuckled.

"C'mon, Josh, I'm serious."

"So what, you think that these three couples are... could be our ghosts? That is, if there are ghosts there... that is, if there really are such things as ghosts, in the first place."

"Think about it!"

"Okay," said Josh. "A bunch of mismatched couples marry and die at this place and we, well, you, actually think the place is being haunted by these same people. Hey! Makes sense to me."

Katie took in a deep breath. "You're right. This is all crazy… Isn't it?

"As I said before, we of all people should know that anyone can see things the way they want to. That's Psych 101. There's probably a very logical explanation for everything we thought happened, yesterday."

"Okay, my love, then call Randy and tell him we're getting married at the Winthrop Manor! And maybe you should mention that we don't intend to die there, also!" And Katie gave Josh a big hug and kiss, almost spilling his tea all over both of them.

Josh put down his cup and put his hands around her neck in a menacing way and said with the voice of Dracula, "Yes, my love. We shall marry there and break the creepy Winthrop curse. Now, my sweet, I must bite your neck!"

He then started sucking on the place right under her left ear.

"Wrong genre, pookie," laughed Katie. "We're talking ghosts, here, not vampires."

"Oh. Right you are. Ah, so how do ghosts sound?"

"Boo!"

"Boo to you, too," said Josh. Then he thought a moment. "But ya know what? Just in case of... whatever... I think I'll do a little googling, myself. A little research on the subject."

"Good googling," she said as she left the room to take a shower. After being up all night, she felt dirty and yucky and suddenly very, very tired. Maybe she would forget the shower and just go back to bed.

Josh immediately sat down at the computer and typed in the Google box, 'Ghosts.'

That same morning found Randy outside the Manor, pruning a hedge with some large shears. Although he was wearing levies and a T shirt, somehow he still looked uptight and conservative. Clothes do not make the man. He looked up and saw his lovely Josie walking across the lawn toward him. Suddenly, he got slightly nervous.

"What're you doing, Randy? Your gardener quit?" she asked, as she approached him with a kiss.

"No, I just thought I'd do a little pruning. I remember I used to love helping my dad when I was a little kid. He had this whole garden out back…"

Laughing, she interrupted him with "… and he smoked most of it, right?"

"I'm not sure he was doing that, then, but don't remind me. I remember growing tomatoes and lettuce, carrots and even corn." Randy half smiled at the memory.

"I don't know, Randy, I just can't picture you as some little hippy tyke in a tie-dyed T shirt and overalls, although you do look quite cute in those jeans."

"Thanks. And well, I was. Got the pictures to prove it."

"Ah, but you shucked your hippy-dippy youth and became Mister Solid Citizen of the world, huh?"

"That's right, I did. I wasn't going to end up like my stoned-out dad. I'm sure my father would probably turn over in his grave if he knew I was a Republican. Thankfully my mom had the sense to take me to Texas where I learned the right and proper things."

"Well, I love you, anyway. So what, you're sprucing up the place for the realtor? Did you ask her to start looking for our little love nest?" And she kissed him on the mouth.

He gently pulled away from her and continued his pruning, only faster, now.

"Randy?"

Almost embarrassed, he didn't answer.

"Randy? What's going on?" Not getting an answer the second time, she took the shears away from him.

Trying to be upbeat he finally said, "You'll never guess! I booked the Manor for a wedding!"

"You did? When?"

"They confirmed this morning and the check's in the mail!"

"No, I mean when's the wedding?"

"Oh. In June. Isn't that the best time for a wedding?"

"But that's months away. I thought you were selling this place and we were getting married. And you said soon."

He ignored her and went on, excitedly. "And the couple, Katie and Josh, they're telling other family members about the place. I think the tides have finally turned for me, Jos."

"Really." Josie didn't like the direction this sea was going.

"Don't worry, Honey, nothing's changed. And really, wouldn't it be better for us if this place finally took off? I mean, who knows how long it might be for it to sell and this way I could, maybe, finally pay off my debts and then we could be married and really start our life together." He was talking faster than he wanted and he knew it.

Anger rose in Josie. "Randy! You're over forty, for crying out loud! Our life should have already started. Three years together and we don't even live together, yet! How long do you expect me to wait?"

Suddenly, Randy looked like a puppy with his tail between his legs, after peeing in the house. "Just a little longer…?"

Josie could only shake her head, sadly. She handed him back the shears and started to walk away from him. Then she stopped and looked down at her engagement ring. She slowly took it off, walked back and handed it to him. Knowing tears were near, she then ran across the lawn.

Randy couldn't believe what had just happened. Why wasn't she happy for him? They would still marry. Why didn't she believe him? He looked down at the ring, then at her running away from him. He thought of running after her, telling her, no, he loved her, wedding bookings or not, he would sell the Manor, they would get married, they would have two kids, a boy, then a girl and they would live happily ever after. But he didn't. Instead, he sadly slipped the ring into his pant's pocket and started pruning again, slowly, then getting faster and faster, until the hedge was nearly destroyed, much like his love life had suddenly become.

CHAPTER TEN

CONTACTING ALL GHOSTS

While Josie holed herself up in her house, leaving only to go to work, then not answering her home phone or her cell when Randy called a million times, he kept himself busy thinking of how to give Josh and Katie the most magnificent day of their lives. He tried not to think about what he had seemingly lost, only what was to be gained by his decision not to put the Manor up for sale at this time. Josie would come to her senses. He knew she would.

A week later the happy couple, with a secret method to their possible madness, came by the Manor to look around again, asking Randy if they might wander the place, alone, to get a better feel for the surroundings.

"Of course!" he told them, happily. "Mi casa is su casa! I'll just be in my office, if you need anything."

They thanked him, then headed straight for the Grand Ballroom. Once there, Katie sat at the long wood bar and took some printed papers out of her briefcase she had brought with her. In fact, they were pages, more aptly, the ghostly research she had printed off her computer. She sat on the high backed-stool and spread her arms out behind her on the bar. Josh, in the meantime, wandered around the large room. It was obvious these two had a plan.

"So, Josh, what do you think about us having tables set up all around the dance floor. I think that would make it cozy. And maybe you and I could be at a table just for two."

"Good idea, Honey. We'll be the center of attention, huh?"

"Well, we had better be. It is our wedding!" she laughed.

Suddenly and without looking behind her, Katie slapped the top of the bar with one of her hands. At the sound, Josh looked at her and they winked to each other.

Katie then got up and walked to him, took him in her arms and they started slow dancing to music only they could hear in their heads.

Katie stood on her tip-toes and whispered in his ear. "What do you think?"

"Let's just keep with the plan, okay?" he whispered back.

For a few moments they danced and snuggled.

"Hey, look at us," Josh said in his regular voice. "I don't think we'll even need a band. Think of the money we'll save."

Katie gave him a gentle love shove. "Don't you just love this room, Honey?"

She looked around her, then up to the ceiling, just in time to see the chandelier start to sway. With her head, she motioned for Josh to look up. He watched the swaying for a moment, then took her by the hand over to the wall where the light switch was and flipped it on. The huge light fixture with it's many, many bulbs went on. Suddenly, it shook harder, as if being scared, that is if an inanimate object could be scared.

Katie slowly walked around the room, seemingly searching for something. Or… someone. In the meantime, Josh walked along the long bar, touching his hand on it as he walked.

"Jack…? Susanna…? Susanna…?" called out Katie, softly.

"Jack? Are you there? We just want to talk to you. …My name's Josh."

"Don't be afraid. Susanna…?"

At this point Katie looked at Josh and wondering what the hell they were doing, they both laughed out loud.

"What're we doing, Josh? I mean, really?"

"Oh, we're just, um, trying to contact some ghosts. No ghosts here? Okay, then."

Still laughing, Katie gathered her ghost papers and stuffed them back into her briefcase. Then Josh took Katie's hand and just as they got to the Grand Ballroom's door, it SLAMMED right in their faces, scaring the crap out of them. They certainly weren't laughing now.

Totally shaken, they could only stare at each other.

"Well," Josh started, "I guess they simply don't want to be contacted, huh?"

Trying to catch her breath, Katie meekly said, "No, no, Josh, I think that was a good sign. A really good sign.." Breathing heavily out of fright, her hand over her quickly beating heart, she paused a moment. "Josh? Do you think they can actually hear us?"

"Well, I think that was either a hurricane type wind that slammed that door, or anything's possible. C'mon, Baby, onward."

Josh slowly and carefully opened the door and they left the ballroom, but not before they both took one last look into the room, where everything was very still.

Next, Katie and Josh climbed the long, circular staircase that led to the master bedroom. They slowly opened the door and tip-toed in, closing the door behind them.

Katie whispered to Josh, "Okay, this is where old man Winthrop and Mildred died. What do you think we should do to, um…"

"…out them?"

Katie had to laugh. "Out them? Out them, Josh? They're ghosts, not gay!"

Just then, the window next to the chair Mildred had breathed her last breath those many years ago, banged closed. Then it opened, then it banged closed again, over and over and over.

Raising her eyebrow in Josh's direction, Katie tentatively walked to the window. She watched it open and close a few times, then she grabbed it when it was open. Suddenly, she was in a fight of her life with an invisible force that tried to close it. It took a minute, but Katie finally won. As if she had won a race, a tennis match, the World Series, she pumped her arms and mouthed, "Yes!" Of course, a moment after that she felt like a complete idiot.

"Mildred? Is that you?" she said in a gentle tone. "Randolph Winthrop? Are you here? We don't want to hurt you."

Josh whispered in her ear, "Good one. We don't want to hurt a friggin' ghost."

"I'm trying to gain their confidence, Josh," she whispered back.

"Okay. Don't move. I'm going to try something." And Josh went over to the huge bed and gently laid himself down on it. And waited. And waited.

Moments later, he half fell off the bed after being goosed.

"Whoa there nelly. Hey, Honey, maybe Mr. Winthrop *is* gay," laughed Josh.

Before Katie had time to warn him, a pillow rose up and hit him hard on the back of his head.

"What the..." Josh spit out as he jumped off the bed into Katie's shaking arms. "Why didn't you warn me?"

"I don't know. I don't know. I saw it, but I didn't believe it. But I saw it. That, that pillow just, ah, well, it just hit you on the head. Just like that. It hit you on the head. Wow."

"I know that, Katie!"

"I feel like we're in the Twilight Zone, Josh. Is this really happening?"

"Well, either that or we're both having the same nightmare."

They both just stood there in each other's arms, trembling.

"Okay. Okay, we have to pull ourselves together, Josh. Ya know what? I think, maybe, they're really, really interacting with us. Whatta you think?"

"Ah, I think if they are, they could be more pleasant about it."

That did it. Josh and Katie started laughing, again.

"Honey, maybe Mr. W. took offense when you said he might be gay."

Josh cleared his throat. "Ah, Mr. Winthrop, Sir, I was just kidding with that gay remark. Although, really, there's nothing wrong with being gay. Believe me, it's now totally acceptable, now, unless, of course you live in a Red state and then you had better think twice before coming out…"

"Josh! Enough! This is no time for a political lecture!" Her mind was racing a mile a minute. "Wait a second. Maybe it's Mildred in the bed and not Mr. Winthrop. Hey, maybe she has the hots for you. Yeah, that makes sense, because whoever was window fighting with me was sure strong."

Just then the window slammed shut, loudly, half scaring the two, almost to death, again

"Let's give them a little while to comprehend what just happened," stated Katie with her therapist voice.

Josh laughed. "Don't you mean let's give *us* a little while to comprehend what just happened?" And he guided her out of the room.

In the hallway, outside the master bedroom, Katie consulted her notes.

"Okay, okay. Ah, let's go to that weeping willow tree. If the newspaper was right, I think that's the place where Heather and Jimmy died."

Minutes later found Katie and Josh sitting under the great weeping willow trying to gather their thoughts and their minds.

"So, you're sure you still want to get married here, Katie? It's not too late to get our deposit back."

"Um… No. I mean, yes. I'm thinking we shouldn't let some silly ghosts stop us."

"But what if they ruin our wedding, Honey?" Josh started laughing. "I mean, really, Katie, what if that dirty old man starts goosing our guests? Or that dirty old woman!"

Seemingly on time, a small branch fell from the tree a few feet away from them. Josh reached for the branch, then looked up at the tree.

"Hey! Is that the best you can do? Who are you? Jimmy? Heather?"

"Josh! Don't be so hostile. You get more with honey... Honey."

By this point the two of them were feeling almost tipsy, giddy. There seemed to be no reality to their lives or what they were doing.

Josh stood up and walked around the tree.

"Hey, man. Jimmy? Ah... Peace, man. Yeah, peace and love, man. Ah... hippy beads. Ah... groovy, dude... Yeah..."

Katie burst out laughing. "What are you doing?!"

"I'm trying to talk to him, in his language. Didn't you say they were hippy folks?"

"Ah, duh, Josh. Hippy beads? They wore them, they didn't *say* them. I mean, uh, I don't know what I mean, but you sound really dumb. Let me try."

Now she got up and walked around the tree.

"Ah, Heather? Listen, I'm sure you're very, very angry at the way you died, here. And it's okay to be angry. I'd be angry, too. You were so young and had so much to live for. I really understand that. I really do."

A few more branches fell from the tree, this time just missing her by a few inches.

"Yes, that's good, Heather. Showing your anger is good."

"Um, Katie? Now what are you doing?" Josh asked.

"Know what just occurred to me? Maybe all these ghosts are taking out their hostilities on us, when they really should be directing them to each other."

Josh thought about that for a moment.

"And ya know what else, Josh? Maybe, just maybe they are still here since they all died, in this... purgatory, so to speak, because of unfinished business they have as couples."

"Mm... very interesting supposition, Madam Freud," he said with a German accent.

She gave him a dirty look. "Okay, smart guy, you have a better explanation?"

"Are you kidding me? We're being attacked on all sides by what might be ghosts, or something, and you want an explanation?" He started laughing, yet again.

"Josh, listen to me. It's hard enough to get *people* to face their demons, much less... dead people. If this is true, maybe we can somehow help."

"Mm, deceased couples therapy." He thinks for a short moment. "Naw, no money in it." And at that they both burst into another laughing siege.

Katie looked at her watch. "Oh, crap! We have to go. I have a patient at two. But I think we should really give all of this some serious thought, Josh."

"I'm thinking," he said as he took her hand and they started toward their car in the parking area.

And then like clock-work, Josh tripped, big time, falling to the ground.

"Okay, stop it!" Josh yelled, as Katie pulled him up.

A few steps later, he tripped again. And then again.

"Is that the best you can do, buddy?! Are you having fun, 'cause you're not scaring me!"

Katie tried her damnedest to hold in her giggles, but finally succumbed, as she held on to Josh, steadying him at every trip, until they got safely to their car.

In the Manor's basement, Jimmy and Randolph One were playing poker at the table, while Jack did pull-ups on an overhead pipe. Three white smoky forms floated into the room and materialized as Mildred, Heather and Susanna.

"There you are, Dear. I've missed you so," said Randolph One, with unmistakable yearning in his voice.

Mildred, as usual, ignored him.

"And what have you guys been up to?" This from Jack.

"We're not guys! We're women! Women! Will you never get it?" shrieked Susanna. "And unlike you three, we've been assessing the situation and trying to figure out what to do!"

"About what?" asked Jimmy, innocently.

"About what? About what?" Heather loudly answered back. "About those two..."

"Katie and Josh," interrupted Mildred.

"Whoever! They're on to us!" continued Heather.

"What exactly does that mean?" This from Randolph One.

"We have no idea, Randolph, but I don't like it," said Heather.

Susanna added, "It's obvious they've done some research..."

"What kind of research?" asked Jack.

"Ya know, Jack, if you took a break from trying to pump up your muscles, you might have noticed the world has changed since you got us killed!" Susanna was pissed.

"It has? How?

"You're an idiot, Jack! I don't know why I ever married you!"

And so it went, the couples fighting, putting each other down and yelling at each other.

Trying to bring some kind of sanity to the conversation, Heather said, "They said something about us, maybe, having unfinished business with each other and facing our demons and maybe that's why we're still here."

"Where, man?" Jimmy asked.

"Are you high, Jimmy? Here! Here!" Now Heather had pretty much had it up to... here, with him

"Ya don't have to get angry, Heather. Are we supposed to be somewhere else?"

"Jesus, Jimmy, I don't know."

"Well, I, for one, am glad I'm here, living again with you, Millie, in our house."

Mildred's eyes were about ready to fall out from all the rolling they did towards her once husband.

"We're not *living*, Randolph One! We're dead! Dead!" Susanna was ready to burst. "We've been floating around this place for an eternity and it just seems to me that there should be something... something else."

"Yeah, like that Peggy Lee song, 'Is That All There is?' put in Heather.

"I never heard of that song," said Mildred.

"Oh, it was a great song. Probably after your time, Mildred," added Heather.

Mildred closed her eyes and dreamily said, "My time. I remember really liking Frank Sinatra. But then that youngin' Elvis person started swiveling his hips. Very nasty."

"Well, I never think about it," said Jimmy, thinking.

"Elvis or Frank Sinatra?"

"No, Mildred. I'm talking about the future. I don't anymore, but I used to think about it all the time, didn't I, Heather?"

"Yeah, unrealistically."

"What's that supposed to mean? I had dreams, Heather. I was gonna be a big singer."

"I wanted to change the world. Make it a better place," said Susanna, sadly.

With bitterness, Jack added, "I just wish I coulda gotten that bastard, Benny The Blimp before he got me. What a great novel I coulda written about my life."

"A noble dream, Jack. A noble dream," said Susanna, sarcasm dripping from her lips.

And Heather admitted to her, "Ya know, Susanna, I wanted to change the world, too."

The two women smiled at each other, bonding them closer than they had been while floating around year after year. It seemed in all that while, none of them ever really talked about important things. The truth was, they simply just floated around and around, day after day after day, never really communicating, telling of their dreams, their past, their pain, their joy. If one might think about it, again, not that different from, need it be said, the living.

Except, that is, for Randolph One, who never let an hour go by without expressing his loss in mournful tones.

"I just wanted you to come back to me, Millie."

"Will you give it up, already? You reaped what you sowed, Randolph One," said Mildred. "I just wanted... I don't know what I wanted," she then admitted, sadly.

And there was quiet in the room, each of the ghosts lost in their own thoughts about their lives, their deaths, where in hell they were and what they might do now.

Then Heather had an idea. "Maybe, we can somehow take control of our lives."

"You mean our deaths, don't you?" This from the always wise Susanna.

"Yeah. Our deaths. I'm really depressed now. I'm going to take a float."

And Heather instantly turned into a white fog and floated away. Jack started doing his pull-ups again, while Jimmy and Randolph One resumed their card game. Mildred and Susanna looked at each other, dissolved into their own white fogs and disappeared.

CHAPTER ELEVEN

SEARCHING FOR THE GHOSTLY TRUTH

Ghosts: "The spirit of a dead person..." "The soul of a dead person. "A disembodied spirit imagined, usually as a vague, shadowy or evanescent form, as wandering among or haunting living persons."

Why Ghosts Haunt: "Supernatural activity inside homes is said to be mainly associated with violent or tragic events in a building's past, such as murder, accidental death and suicide." "Seen where pain and suffering occurred for a certain individual."

But why do some dead folks with bad, sad, unfortunate pasts become ghosts, while others don't? This and other ghostly questions might never be answered unless some very intelligent ghost, uh, maybe, eventually gets reincarnated, remembers their past life and/or death and writes a best selling novel, or better yet, a self help tome, goes on Oprah or Regis and Kelly and discusses the subject at great length.

A better question might be, what to do with ghosts, when and if we find them lurking in our closet? No, wait! That was a nightmare, not a ghost in your closet. But could what one thinks to be a nightmare, really be a ghost? Or... vice-versa?

What to do? What to do when we truly believe there are ghosts among us? Should we bust them? Should we try and communicate with them? Should we simply ignore them? Should we do an in-depth study of them to see if, in fact, they really do exist? And if we believe in our heart of hearts they exist, does it mean they really do? If Santa Claus and the Easter Bunny and the Tooth Fairy are real, why not ghosts! Are ghosts inherently bad? Or perhaps, inherently good? Are ghosts the same as those friendly folks those TV psychics like to talk to, or is that just your kind old Aunt Martha come back to say 'hi'... and oh yeah, 'your mother's antique ring you thought you lost forever is really under your pink thong underwear in the left, top drawer of your bureau.'

Getting back to the ghosts of Winthrop Manor, were they really haunting prospective soon-to-be married couples, or haunting each other, psychologically speaking, transferring all their own marital woes onto others? So many questions, so little time.

And time was something Katie and Josh felt they were running out of before their own wedding, that is, if they wanted to celebrate their day of days at the Winthrop Manor in peace and love and harmony. They were going to get to the bottom of this ghost thing, if it was the last thing they did.

And so it was that one fine sunny, Southern California spring day found Katie and Josh sitting in the shabby office of one Alvin Putty, a strange, little, eccentric and rather maniacal looking person.

"Mr. Putty…" started Josh.

"Please, call me Alvin," said the beady-eyed man.

"Okay. Alvin. We think, now, of course, we don't know, because honestly the idea is almost too insane to imagine, but we think we might have, shall we say, come in contact with, ah… well…" Josh had his fishing pole out for the right word, but his hook had lost it's worm.

"Say it! Ghosts! That's why you're here, isn't it?" There seemed to be unbridled glee in the man's voice.

"Well, Mr. Putty... Alvin, we're not sure. Logically, it just couldn't be true, but, we just, ah, think..." Katie wanted to use the right words, also, in her explanation.

Alvin relished interrupting Katie. "Denial! Denial!"

"Denial?" she questioned.

"Of course! We mortals don't like to think these evil entities exist, that what we *know* to be true, what we experienced, we justify as only our wild imagination! That's their insidious nature! They manipulate our minds until we think we are going crazy! Crazy! And then they... strike!! Evil doers, all of them!" Alvin Putty had whipped himself into a frenzy.

"Well, I don't think these ones, if they are... ones, are really evil," said Katie trying to sound calm.

"No, Alvin, they really don't seem evil at all. Inept, perhaps, but certainly not evil," Josh added.

"Are you crazy?! Of course they're evil! And they must be destroyed!" Now Alvin was sweating down his neck.

"Ah, Sir, what exactly do you mean by... destroyed?" Josh was getting a very weird feeling about this nutcase across the desk from him.

"Destroyed! Annihilated! Gone! Poof!"

"Poof?" Katie couldn't take her eyes off Mr. Alvin Putty. And no, she certainly wasn't putty in his hands.

Alvin stood up, puffed out his five feet two inch frame and bellowed, "Destroyed! Poof! And I'm the one to do it!"

He then walked over to a book shelf where sat a large Plexiglas container, inside of which was a heavy box-shaped contraption with a gun-looking projectile coming out of one end. He lifted it out of its case and pointed it right at Josh. "Poof!"

Dumbfounded and momentarily mute, Katie and Josh could only stare from the contraption to Alvin Putty, from Alvin Putty back to the contraption.

"I know, I know, you're at a loss for words, folks, but I am the number one ghost buster on the West Coast! Now, where did you say these ghosts reside? I can take care of them as quick as you can blink an eye.

Blink an eye they did and quickly excused themselves, never to lay eyes on Mr. Alvin Putty again, at least in this life, and hopefully, not in the hauntingly next one.

"O-kay, that was scarier than anything we've encountered at the Winthrop Manor," Katie told Josh as they walked to their car.

"Ya bet your bippy, it was," retorted Josh.

They both started to laugh, somewhat nervously, as they plotted where to go next to find some answers.

And next, was the Séance Room of the distinguished old psychic, Madam Zola. The room was lit only by candles. Around a small table, draped with an old, fringed cloth, a large crystal ball in the center, sat Katie, Josh and Madam Zola. Madam Zola looked like she might be one's old Russian bubbe, grandmother for you non-Jewish folks. She was dressed in a peasant shirt and long skirt, her head wrapped in a scarf. Truthfully, she looked like she just got off the boat at Ellis Island a century before. Her Russian accent was so thick, it was sometimes hard to understand her.

"So, my children, who might it be that it is that you would like to contact?"

Katie leaned over to Josh and whispered, "Isn't a psychic already supposed to know?"

Josh just shrugged.

"Ah, well, is anyone coming... ah... through?" Josh innocently asked.

First Madam Zola put her arthritic hands on the crystal ball, massaging it. Then she dramatically threw her head back, rolling her eyes to what seemed to be inside of her head. Then she jerked her head to the right. Then to the left. She then dropped her head forward, back again, forward, back, forward, then she looked straight ahead, as if in a trance.

It took every ounce of strength in Katie and Josh's bodies not to get hysterically laughing.

"Shhh! Yes! Yes! Someone is coming through! A woman! Does that make any sense to either of you?"

"Ah, do you think you could be just a little more specific, Madam?" Josh asked while rolling his eyes upward, inside of his own head, hoping her trance was so deep she didn't notice.

"Listen, I just tell it as I see it. It's a woman, that's for sure."

Suddenly she looked over her shoulder, as if looking straight at someone.

"What...? Really...? No kidding..."

Who in hell was she talking to, Katie and Josh wondered, when Madam Zola quickly turned back to them.

"A violent death! Not of her own making. She's telling me... What? ... She's telling me, 'water, water!' So, kids, how am I doing?"

"Ah... no. Nothing. Sorry. Josh?" asked Katie.

"No, me neither. Water, huh? No."

"Oh… " Madam Zola sounded depressed.

Suddenly, her head again jerked and she started twitching all over.

"Wait! Wait!. Yes! I see an old man. A very old man."

And just as suddenly she got Katie and Josh's attention, again.

"An old man? Really?" asked Katie, hoping, hoping. She was now leaning over the table, closer to Madam Zola.

"Yes. A very old man who… who… dies."

"How? How does he die? Where does he die?" asked Josh, anticipation oozing out of him.

"Ah… wait… he said… he said, he dies… from… hmm, that's very strange…"

"What?!" Josh and Katie screamed out together.

"I hear buzzing. Buzzzzz… Buzzing, all around me. Buzz, buzz, buzz." Madam Zola started swatting away imaginary bees with her old hands.

Katie slumped back in her chair. "Buzzing bees? That's how he dies? What? He's stung to death?"

"Yes, yes, that's right. Stung to death. Until dead. Stung. Oy, it was terrible, he tells me. But he says that death was welcome and that he's at peace now in heaven…" A pregnant

146

pause and then, "Wait, wait!" and Madam Zola laughs a hearty laugh. "Yes, yes, good…. I'm glad, yes…. He says he is very happy to tell all of us that there are no bees in heaven."

Josh and Katie could only look at each other, knowing if they sat there another minute they would both pee in their pants.

The frustrated lovebirds were getting nowhere, so as a last resort, it was back to the Google. Who knew so much was written, thought up, made up, surmised about ghosts?

One web site told them some very interesting facts: Ghosts want to be noticed. Well, that was true. Ghosts have no sense of passing time. Often they don't know they're dead. Ghosts can smell things and love the smell of lemons. They have a sense of humor and love to hear humans laugh. Most ghosts are happy, but some still cling to an emotional pain. They are pranksters. Ghosts can read your thoughts. Ghosts retain all the memories and emotions of their lives. Sometimes ghosts are trapped and need to be released and one should let them know they can move on. If a spirit was a jerk while living, they will probably still be a jerk while a ghost. Ghosts make friends with other ghosts from different eras. Most ghosts can't or won't hurt you. If you're being haunted, if you simply ask them to leave, they will. Say something like,

'I know you are here, but you are scaring me, please leave.'

Katie and Josh found all this information quite fascinating. What they didn't or couldn't have known is how so much of this was true.

Another web site, Ghost Truth, saw the truth of ghosts in an entirely different fashion. "… Even so-called friendly ghosts are dangerous! Yes, dangerous! Demons and/or evil spirits are in reality the fallen angels who were cast out of heaven along with Lucifer and who love to masquerade as our departed loved ones, weird ghosts and troublesome poltergeists. Fallen angels are very real and very evil. They love to deceive and are Lucifer's army of evil ones. .."

Katie and Josh decided the first site was much more believable. At least they wanted to, hoped that it was closer to the truth. Josh decided whoever was tripping him, probably Jimmy, was, in fact, a jerk. Since the couples were from different decades, Katie wondered if they had all made friends with each other. The sentence that affected both Josh and Katie the most was, "Sometimes ghosts are trapped and need to be released. Let them know they can move on."

But why were they trapped? And what might it be that would release them? And if they were to move on, where would they go? So many questions. But Katie had come to a conclusion. She believed with all her heart, even before all their research about the Winthrop ghosts, if that's what they were, and about ghosts in general, that perhaps the problem really was, that these three couples who died in unhappy circumstances, had never worked out their problems with each other. Heck, that was enough to keep an unhappy couple living in a black purgatory of a lousy relationship while living on earth, miserable, she thought. And now it was her quest in life to somehow actually contact the ghosts, to help them to work out their problems and hopefully then move on. No more fighting a window that kept opening and closing, No more slapping something that slapped them on the bar. No more getting goosed, that was for sure.

Josh, of course, thought it might be a completely nutty idea, but Katie was on a mission and nothing was going to stop her. But who to try and contact first?

CHAPTER TWELVE

CONTACT! CONTACT!

Katie sat pondering. And then she pondered some more. Who would, should she try and contact? Just the thought of that sounded crazy to her. Contact ghosts? Really? Really, really? It sounded to her like contacting aliens. If it could possibly happen, would it be the way it was when Drew Barrymore first saw ET? They would look at each other and both start screaming their lungs out? Or would it be more like the night when Richard Dreyfuss hid in the mountains overlooking the alien landing sight in Close Encounters Of the Third Kind? Suddenly that distinct synthesizer music from the movie started going round and round in her head and wouldn't stop. Then she thought of the horrifying film, Alien, remembering how that thing, that ugly thing burst forth from Sigourney Weaver's body. Yuck! She went over to her kitchen sink and threw cold water on her face. No, she wasn't going to be contacting aliens, she was going to try to contact ghosts. Less scary? Less insane? She thought not.

But which one? She looked over her printed computer papers with pictures of the three couples. How sweet Mildred looked as an old woman, sweeter still as a beautiful young, newly married woman, in that sepia toned photo. But what would she have in common with a woman so many generations back? Susanna was beautiful. A Communist activist, a rebel rouser. Maybe. And then there was the lithe spirit, Heather. She stared at the photo of the girl with flowers in her hair. Was she going to San Francisco? Now that song swam around in her brain. Heather was in Katie's own mother's generation. She knew more about the 70's than she did the other decades. For goodness sake, Katie had been born into that generation, although her parents were far from being hippies or ever attending love-ins.

Yes! It would be Heather she would try and contact. When she told Josh of her decision, he heartedly agreed, even though he was still somewhat skeptical that even if these ghosts were real, for lack of a better word, was there a way to get through to them? He was also leery of the fact that Katie wanted to go out to the Manor by herself. If they were ghosts, were they just warming up with a falling branch here or a swaying chandelier there? Would his love be in danger?

But Katie stood firm. After all, he and the police, for that matter, would only be a cell call away if anything dangerous were to happen, that is, as long as it wouldn't be too late by the time they got there. She readily put any thought of imminent danger out of her mind, a mind she admitted, she might well already be out of.

"Don't even think I could be in danger, Josh! You're freaking out an already freaked out person.! I'm doing this!"

"Okay, but just make sure Randy is somewhere around."

"I will. Don't worry. Just not too close around."

That settled, Katie pondered on. She wanted to make Heather feel as comfortable as possible. She didn't want to come on in any threatening way. But she couldn't stop thinking about what she was about to do, about to try to do. The whole thing was so inconceivable, she finally decided to stop thinking and just go with the flow. And so, on the morning of the day that she would hopefully *not* meet her Maker, but a friendly ghost, instead, she took a lot of time and thought in the process of getting ready.

After taking a warm morning bath, she doused herself in lemon oil she had bought the day before. Hadn't that internet site said that ghosts liked the smell of lemons? Come to think about it, she liked it, too and decided to change perfumes from her usual Egyptian Musk to lemon oil, from this day forth. Next were her clothes. Her rather conservative therapist clothes wouldn't do at all. Luckily she still had in her closet an outfit she had worn the year before on Halloween, faded, torn levis, a T shirt stating 'Make Love Not War, sandals on her feet, a peace necklace and large feathered earrings. Josh had thought she had made one hot hippy.

All dressed, she looked in her full-length mirror. Not bad, she said to herself. She considered wearing a headband around her forehead, but thought that might be overdoing it just a little. The funny thing was, she saw kids on the street wearing similar outfits on the streets, everyday. No, for years, now, this was no costume. What was old was new, again and this made her feel more comfortable in her ripped jeans.

Josh walked into their bedroom, looked at her, made the fingers on his right hand into a 'V' and said, "Peace."

"Very funny. So, how do I look?"

"Groovy."

They both laughed, kissed and then Katie was on her way to hopefully meet a ghost. On the drive up to the Winthrop Manor and to really get into the mood, Katie played old tapes of Jackson Browne and The Eagles. The music transported her back to a time she never knew, but now would have loved to live in. It was only when she parked her car and started her trek across the great lawn toward the weeping willow that her nerves kicked in, again.

Damn, she thought. Randy was sitting under the weeping tree.

"Hey," he said, sounding sad.

"Hey, Randy. Are you okay? You did remember I was coming to look around, again, didn't you?"

"Oh, yeah. I was just sitting here."

She sat down on the ground next to him.

"Are you sure you're okay? You don't look so good."

"Sure. Yeah. And stay as long as you'd like and feel free to come in, if you want, too."

"I might do that. Thanks."

Being the therapist she was, she was sure something was wrong with this man, when he continued sitting, lost in thought.

"Randy, are you sure you're okay?"

"Oh, yeah. By the way, did you tell your relatives about maybe booking my place for, what was it, an anniversary or something?"

"Oh, no. Not yet. Things have been so crazy getting ready for our wedding, but I will."

Randy tried to hide his disappointment, but failed.

"I will. I promise. You really don't look so good."

"No, it's nothing. Just having some girlfriend stuff going on, that's all. Not a big deal."

"Well, you know I'm a therapist, if you want to talk about anything."

"Me? Therapy? I don't think so."

Katie laughed lightly. "No, I just mean I might be able to give you some insights. You're going to be giving us this beautiful wedding, it's the least I can do. My little thank you."

"That's very nice of you, but, no thanks." And he was silent a moment or two. Then... "Well, see, my girlfriend, Josie, she wants to get married and I, I guess I just don't feel, I don't know, that I'm worthy of her, right now. There's all this stuff in my life I feel I have to straighten out first, ya know?"

Katie looked at the nice looking man and saw his pain.

"Well, one thing I know is if you love her, make that your priority, Randy. I really believe that in this life, nothing is more important than love. In an instant we could be gone, you know? If you really love her, don't make that relationship a lost opportunity. Really. I believe love is more important than anything else in this world. And losing it might, well, haunt you for the rest of your life."

Katie was well aware of her words and she was hoping if Heather was around, she might be listening, also.

"Wow. I'll think about that. Thanks, Katie. Yeah, I'll think about that. Thanks, again."

She smiled warmly at him as he got up and started back toward the Manor. Then Katie looked up at the weeping willow and took a deep breath. Leaning back on the trunk of the tree, the branches waved slightly in the breeze. She took another deep breath.

"Ah... Heather? Heather, are you there? Here? ...Okay, I really feel stupid talking out loud to... no one. Unless, of course, you're here. Are you here, Heather?"

To say Katie felt stupid was actually a gross understatement. She couldn't believe she was actually doing this. What could she have been thinking? Even if these folks were ghosts, why would anyone in their right mind think they could communicate with the living, in any way, shape or form. But she would not be deterred.

"Ya know, Heather, I actually think we have a lot in common, you and me. I read you were getting your Masters, that you wanted to go into politics and, ah, and after you... died, your mother was quoted as saying how you wanted to change the world and how you marched against the war and for women's rights and civil rights. She was so proud of you, Heather."

Just then a small gust of wind blew through the weeping willow. Katie noticed it, but didn't react.

"Wow, if you think there was something to march for back then, you wouldn't believe how crazy the world is now. I was thinking of going into politics, too, at one point, but decided to become a therapist, instead..."

As she continued talking, a white, foggy form floated down from the tree, that Katie couldn't see.

"Ya know, my passion is helping people. Heather? Maybe I could help you."

So very softy, almost unheard, coming from behind the tree, Katie could have sworn she heard a woman's voice say, "Help me? Help me how?"

She slowly turned her head around, her heart beating a mile a minute, but saw nothing. Trembling, Katie tried to compose herself. Was her mind just playing tricks on her? Did she think she heard a voice, because she wanted to, so much?

"Ah... well... well... you know, there's always a reason for everything. I really believe that. Maybe there's even a reason you're still here... if you are here. Are you here, Heather?"

She listened intently for another word. For something, but there was only quiet and the soft chirping of a bird in the tree.

"I'm not here to hurt you, Heather. I just want to talk to you, that's all... I know, I know, this is all nuts. It's crazy. I mean, how do you think I feel, sitting here, talking to myself, thinking maybe, maybe a ghost might be listening?"

And then she heard it. Or she thought she heard it. Yes! She was positive she heard her name being called, ever so softly.

"Katie...?"

If one might think Katie was nervous, that was nothing to how Heather was feeling. She had heard Katie talking with Randy and something really hit home with her when Katie talked about love and relationships. And when she heard what her mother had said after she had died, it brought tears to Heather's eyes. She hadn't thought about her mother, her family, it seemed like forever. Why hadn't she thought about her life and all the good times she had had growing up with her family, since she had died? Why did it seem the only thing she thought of while floating around all these years was just how angry she was at Jimmy, how angry she was at dying so young, how all of her dreams remained unfulfilled?

"Katie…?" This time Heather's voice was stronger.

Katie's eyes widened, this time knowing that she heard her name being called.

"I'm here. Right here. Where are you? Are you Heather?"

Suddenly sensing something she didn't have a word for, Katie turned her head and saw the lovely Heather, who had slowly materialized from her white foggy self, standing next to her, the flowers in her hair still fresh. Trying to keep her cool, now wondering if she had fallen asleep and this was just a dream, Katie stood up and faced the girl.

"Heather…?"

"Hi…"

It was hard to tell who was more nervous, giddy.

"Oh my God! Heather?!"

"You can really see me?"

Katie started laughing in a completely nervous and excited way.

"I can see you! I can see you! Look at you! You look just like the photo in the paper. Oh wow. I can see you. Is it really you?"

Heather looked at Katie, amazed, then down at her own body. "Wow, I didn't know I could do that! This is, this is crazy!"

And for a few minutes the two just stared at each other. Then Heather put out her hand and touched Katie's arm.

"I can feel you, too!" Then she laughed. "Nice shirt. Nice outfit."

Katie was suddenly embarrassed. "Okay, I dressed this way because I thought it might make you feel... more at home. But honestly, kids are dressing this way, again... Holy crap, I'm talking to a ghost I can see and we're discussing fashion!"

They both laughed.

Heather took in a deep, deep breath. She felt almost... alive.

"Mm... you smell good."

"It's lemon oil."

"That's funny or weird or something. I never liked the smell of lemon, when I was... well, you know. But I guess I do now." And she leaned closer to Katie and took another breath. "Mm, nice."

Funny, indeed. Katie didn't tell her about that ghost list she had found on the internet saying ghosts liked the smell of lemon.

And so it was that Katie and Heather sat under the weeping willow for a long, long while talking about all sorts of things. What had happened in the world the past thirty years. Fads. Movies. Politics. Everything except the real reason Katie was there and the real reason Heather was there. Soon they were just two young women chatting, almost forgetting that one of them was alive and the other dead. Just two girlfriends yakking away. And then the talk turned to the serious, the present, the real reason for this happening.

"I know we've made our presence felt to people, but I never in a million years figured someone, you know, alive could ever *see* us," Heather said, never once taking her eyes off Katie.

"Maybe it was time."

"Maybe it was... is," agreed Heather. "You said something last time you were here that really affected me, that maybe we're still around because of some kind of unfinished business."

Katie became very professional, all of a sudden, the therapist in her coming out. "That's right. Even, ah, we... earthlings... people.... don't, can't move
forward until we work out that business."

This got Heather laughing.

"What?" asked Katie.

"Ya know, we did have therapy back in my time."

"Oh, of course you did," said an embarrassed Katie.

"EST was really the 'in' thing to do."

"Yeah, I read about that."

"It was a load of crap! You'd go to these two day seminars and they wouldn't let you even pee the whole time. Breaking you down, then supposedly building you up, again. The only thing that was built up was the pee in your bladder! Urinary infections were very big back then."

And they both laughed.

Hours went by quickly as the two women never seemed to run out of things to talk about. And then finally...

"So, Heather, do you think the others will be into it, talking to us?"

"I don't know. Jimmy always hated the idea of seeing a shrink. He said it was for sissies."

"Well, he hasn't tripped me yet. He is the tripper, isn't he."

"Oh, yeah," Heather laughed. "No, he's probably in the basement playing poker with Randolph One."

"Poker?"

"Hey, even ghosts get bored, ya know." And she laughed, again.

It seemed to Heather that she had laughed more this day than she had in the more than three decades since she died and she liked the feeling of it.

"I'm going to talk to all of them about meeting you and you maybe being able to help us. Wow, they're gonna to flip out. But one thing I do know and that's that Randolph One would do anything to get his Millie back. That's what he calls her. She's so sad and angry all the time. I know therapy wasn't something folks did back in their generation, that much."

"It sounds like all of you are sad and angry. Maybe we *can* help you, guys. Wow, I can't wait for Josh to meet you!"

"He's very cute. You two seem really happy, together."

"We are. He's my honey."

"But, Katie, if you can help us, then what? What do you think will happen to us?"

"I don't know, Heather. I don't know..."

It was a while later when the two were walking around the great lawn, that Randy happened to look out his office window. What he saw was an animated Katie walking and seemingly talking and laughing to herself. It was truly the oddest sight, he thought he had ever seen. He kept staring at her.

"Great. A therapist who talks to herself. That's just great."

CHAPTER THIRTEEN

THERAPY SHMARAPY

Randy had never been in therapy. It just wasn't something he had ever even considered doing. And although what Katie had told him that afternoon had struck a cord with him, "... if you love her, make that your priority... I really believe in this life, there is nothing more important than love..." seeing her on the lawn, talking, laughing, making wild arm gestures, well, maybe it was Katie who needed therapy, not him. And yet, it got him thinking about his life and what was really important 'in this life.' Yes, he wanted to make something of himself. Yes, he wanted to make a success out of the Winthrop

Manor, his namesake. But at what cost? He knew he loved Josie and didn't want to lose her.

And so that evening a very nervous Randolph Winthrop The Fourth walked up to his love's duplex and rang the bell. He didn't know what he was going to say, exactly, or how he was going to say what he didn't know what he was going to say, but he knew it was time to say something.

Josie had been curled up on her couch reading, but the words she read just seemed to pass by her brain. She was thinking about Randy and how much time she felt she had wasted on their relationship. Enough was enough. If this man, whom she did love, couldn't commit to her after all these years, well then, she would commit herself to something or someone else. Josie was sad then mad then sad then mad, again. And that's when her doorbell rang.

Looking through the front door peephole, her eye seeing only part of his face, Josie's heart made a sort of flop-flop. Was he there to beg for her forgiveness? Was he there to tell her he didn't love her, anymore?

"What're you doing here, Randy?" she asked, through her wooden door.

"I just wanted to talk to you, Josie."

"You could have called."

"I wanted to see you."

"I don't know what there is to talk about, Randy. You made your position perfectly clear."

"No, Josie. I was just so excited when I finally got that wedding." And then he begged and begged until she let him in.

For a long while, he made his case, again and again, how he just felt he had nothing to offer her. How he felt like such a loser. How the Winthrop Manor was his legacy and how, yes, he had become obsessed with making it a success, making the Winthrop name something to be respected again. And he admitted that if he failed, then what would he have to offer her as a man, as a husband, eventually as a father to their children. And hard as it was, he told her he felt like a nothing, just like his father had been. A nothing.

"I just don't feel I have anything, anything to offer you, Josie" And he put his head down, afraid that tears were close in coming.

"Randy! You have you! That's all I ever wanted. You! I don't need a big house to live in. I don't need loads of money. I don't care about those things."

"But I just thought by waiting until…"

"Until what, Randy? Who knows, we could be dead tomorrow! Then we would have wasted our whole damn life that we could have been together!"

"Yeah…" Randy said, thinking again of Katie's words to him. '… losing love might haunt you the rest of your life.'

"I want to live, now, Randy. I just want to live now, with you."

And so they talked and talked and even cried a little, together and it was quite therapeutic for both of them. In the end Randy decided to put the Manor up for sale right after Katie and Josh's wedding. And to celebrate, they decided to go away up the coast the next weekend for a romantic few days. Randy knew in his heart of hearts it was the right thing to do, that he had finally made the right decision.

In the master bedroom of the Winthrop Manor, the ghosts were discussing therapy and should they or should they not all materialize, so that Katie and Josh could look into their individual psyches, analyze them and hopefully be of help.

Mildred sat in her chair, the others on the bed, while Heather regaled them about her unbelievable afternoon with Katie and how the real live woman could actually see her and talk to her. But most of the others remained skeptical, to say the least. Even Susanna, at first, thought Heather was making the whole thing up. It took some convincing on Heather's part, but finally they all did remember Katie and Josh calling out their names and trying to interact with them. But there was still resistance.

"I'm not having my head shrunk!" said Jimmy.

"Yeah, it's small enough as it is," laughed Jack.

Jimmy immediately punched Jack in the arm.

"They want to shrink our heads, Mille? No, no, I don't want my head shrunk. That's a terrible idea," said a nervous Randolph One.

Mildred, yet again, rolled her eyes at him.

"It's just an expression, Randolph One. Therapists are sometimes called 'shrinks.' But they're really interested in helping people, bringing out truths, expanding their minds."

"They're gonna give us some LSD? Cool." This joking, of course, from Jimmy.

"LDS? What's that?" Jack asked.

"LSD! Oh, man, you lived in the wrong decade, Jack. You want to expand your mind, forget therapy. Psychedelics, that's the way to go! You see the world in, like, a totally different dimension."

"Yeah, Jimmy and because of your 'expanded mind' we left this world. Idiot!" It was hard for Heather to even look at her husband, at that moment.

"Oh come on, Heather, I was only smoking some weed that day and you know it."

Mildred looked at them as if they were speaking a foreign language. "What are you all talking about, children?"

"Nothing, Mildred. Let's get back to the issue at hand," said Susanna. "Why not? What harm could it do? I vote to talk to these people."

"I second the motion!" agreed Heather

"I'm the head of this household and I make the decisions around here!" Randolph One yelled out.

"You always did, didn't you? And look where it got you. You're a very bad decision maker. So not this time, old man. I vote with the girls," said a suddenly empowered feeling Mildred.

"Mildred!" the two women exclaimed at the same time.

Susanna and Heather immediately went and stood behind Mildred. All together for the common good.

"That's right! I vote with the girls! Women!" said the happier than usual old woman, although she had no idea what the consequences of this voting might entail. But at that moment she didn't care.

And then there was silence in the room, all of them wondering the how's and where's and why's of what they were possibly about to do.

"Okay, fine, but what if then things change?" said Jack.

"Yeah, man. What if?" Jimmy asked.

'And what if things *don't* change?" asked Heather. "I'm tired of all of this. I'm tired of this life. This… death. All we do is feebly scare couples over and over and over again. Maybe any change would be good, better, whatever that change is. I'm telling you guys, it was so bitchin' talking with Katie. I felt… alive, again."

"What is this 'bitchin' thing, Heather?" asked Mildred.

"Oh, Mildred, it's just another expression. It means good," explained an amused Heather.

"Bitchin'. Bitchin'!" I like that word," laughed Mildred. "Bitchin'!"

"So, let's just do it. What do we have to lose, huh? Maybe it'll be poppycock. Maybe nothing will change, but let's do it!" said Susanna.

"Poppycock! Bitchin'. Bitchin' poppycock!" said Mildred happily, almost child-like.

And even the men had to laugh.

"Okay, okay, I'm the man of this house and I say… fine. Let's talk to them."

"Randolph One, who's side are you on?" asked a pissed Jack.

"Ah, man, One!" said Jimmy.

Randolph One leaned over to Jimmy and Jack on the bed and whispered out of the side of his mouth, "Boys, they'll make our life hell if we don't agree. Let's just play along with their little game and get it over with... Okay, girls, you win. Heather, set up the meeting."

Funny thing about ghosts, they don't think the way humans do. They don't necessarily see the ramifications of their actions. Day merges into night merges into day. They don't understand why they are here or there, for that matter. They just, more or less, exist. And it seems to take some extraordinary circumstance to change that existence. At least that seemed to be the case for the ghosts of Winthrop Manor. Funny, also, was the fact that it was the women who held onto their anger, their sadness, while the men seemed okay with the status quo, playing cards and staying in shape, doing some tripping and swaying and goosing, agreeing to do these silly things, only to try and stay in their women's good graces. Oh yes, Randolph One moaned and groaned about wanting his Millie back, but he was never able to take any responsibility for the reason she left him in the first place. Perhaps there wasn't that much of a difference between the males and females who walked this earth and those who floated it.

As prearranged with Heather, Katie trekked back up to the Manor a few days later, to see what Heather's ghost comrades thought. The historic meeting was planned for that weekend. This time when the lovely she-ghost materialized at the weeping willow, Katie took it in her stride, as if it were the most natural of happenings. Both women were excited, yet nervous, having no idea what to expect.

Again, from his office window, Randy watched Katie talking and laughing to herself. Maybe this woman was a little nuts, but he had to admit, because of her he had other things on his mind, that being his romantic weekend with Josie. For a man who kept his feelings in check, the thought of being with Josie, again, sent giddy chills up and down his spine, not to mention parts of his body that shall remain nameless.

Changes seemed to be coming for everyone and everything at the Winthrop Manor. The land began to ready itself for springtime and rebirth. Seeds dormant through the winter were preparing to push forth from the earth into new life. A new beginning was at hand. Of course, one never knows how new beginnings will end.

Tiny blades of grass poked up from the ground and new baby green leaves on the trees could be seen beginning to cover the barren branches in the park where Katie and Josh were jogging.

"So, Honey, are you ready for tomorrow?" asked Josh, breathing heavily from the physical exertion.

"I can't wait," huffed and puffed an excited Katie.

"I know, but we just can't have too many expectations, you know?"

"I know. How can you have expectations of something you absolutely can't believe in the first place?" laughed Katie.

They stopped their jogging and sat down on a park bench. They both grabbed for bottled water out of their fanny packs and took a few long gulps.

"This is totally bizarre, you know that, don't know? We're treading on very weird waters, here," said Josh.

"I know, Josh, but after actually meeting Heather, I just want her to be happy. She's so great. You're going to adore her. Talking with her, it was almost as if she were alive, just like you and me."

"Katie, considering the circumstances, do you think we'll even know what could make her or the others happy?"

"Happiness is universal!" said Katie

"Okay, I'll buy that. But are they even in our universe?" asked Josh.

"Ya know what? I'm not even going to think of anything rationally, 'cause none of this is rational. We're going to go up there and meet a bunch of hopefully nice folks, who just happen to be ghosts and try and help them!" And she set off running, not jogging, this time.

Josh got up and tried to catch her.

CHAPTER FOURTEEN

THE COAST IS CLEAR FOR LOVE

'… The dream, the hope, things planned, or seen, or wrought.
Companion, comforter and guide and friend,
As much as love asks love, does thought ask thought.
Life is so short, so fast the lone hours fly,
We ought to be together, you and I.'

> Henry Alford

Ah, the poems of love… 'How do I love thee, let me count the ways…,' '…I love you, not only for what you are, but for what I am when I am with you…,' '…For the mist, if it comes, and the weeping rain, will be changed by the love into sunshine again.'

But what the hell is love, anyway? Not how one feels when they're in love. Not what love seemingly does to a person? What *is* it?! There are hundreds upon hundreds of definitions for love. A warm feeling. Deep affection for another. Devotion. The relation between sweethearts. The romantic or sexual relationship between two people. That warm, fuzzy feeling when you are near to another person. When one's heart is aflutter at the mere thought of another. When that ruby red organ in one's chest feels like it will explode with joy. With all that has been written about love, does anyone really know what it is? The answer is a resounding... NO! Perhaps it's simply a feeling that has no definition, whatsoever.

It was a sparkling and gloriously clear day as Randy and Josie drove up the coast to Santa Barbara. The waters of the Pacific were blue as blue could be, dotted with sail boats that bobbed up and down the whitecaps in the gentle waves.

"I'm so glad we're doing this," said Randy, as he reached over to take Josie's hand.

"Me, too."

But the truth was, Josie wasn't sure that Randy could really change his priorities, that she would finally become more important to him than that big, old house.

"I love you, Josie."

"I know that, Randy."

Uh, oh, thought Randy. It's always a bad sign when a person professes love for another and the other doesn't immediately return with a gushing, "I love you, too." But he said nothing and just squeezed her hand in a loving way.

As they got closer to their destination, a quaint Bed And Breakfast near the water, Randy racked his brain trying to think of ways he could truly prove to Josie his love for her. He was feeling so desperate, he decided he would become a Democrat just to please her. How better for anyone, even a fiscally conservative Republican, such as he, to prove their undying love? Ironically, at that very moment Josie was mulling over in her head things she loved and didn't love about him. 'Jeez, if only he were more liberal in his thinking,' she thought. Maybe this weekend, she would expound on all the virtues of being a liberal.

They were rather quiet the rest of the trip, besides every now and again commenting on how beautiful the ocean was, how nice it was to get away, what movie they might go and see that night and other mundane conversation.

Once settled in their room discussion led to how to spend the rest of the day. Randy suggested walking State Street, the main drag of Santa Barbara, maybe taking in the small art museum there. Josie mentioned perhaps driving up to the old Mission. And back and forth they went.

"Roller skating!" said Josie, finally.

"Rolling skating? Really?"

"C'mon, Randy. It'll be fun. Whizzing along next to the ocean. Fresh air! Exercise!"

"I don't whiz, Josie."

"You don't whiz?" she laughed.

He finally admitted that he had only been on roller skates twice in his life, the second time falling and spraining his ankle so badly, he was in a cast for three weeks.

"Ahh, poor baby. Well, don't worry, I'll hold you up. C'mon, it'll be fun!"

Maybe if he agreed to go skating, then he wouldn't have to change his political affiliation, after all, he thought. How much is one expected to do for love, anyway? But the idea of being on skates terrified him possibly even more than voting for a blue Donkey, so still he hemmed and hawed.

"Okay, if you want to sit in this room all afternoon, suit yourself, but I'm going skating!" Josie adamantly told him.

Less than half an hour later, he was sitting on a bench with Josie, lacing up the patriotic red and blue skates he had rented. Josie, possibly showing off, tied up her skates first and did a few perfect pirouettes in front of him.

"Very pretty," he said as he struggled to get up.

They certainly didn't whiz down the skating path that was for sure. Randy held onto Josie for dear life, not really skating, but rather shuffling one foot in front of the other.

"You're doing great, Randy!"

"I'm making a fool out of myself."

"No you're not. And I'm very proud of you. A lot of guys wouldn't even try something they weren't good at."

He looked up at her with love, instead of at his feet and almost went flying.

"I'm such a klutz. This is embarrassing, Josie."

"No, I think you're getting the hang of it, now."

And so they shuffled on.

"Thank you for going away with me this weekend, Jos. For giving me another chance," he said, as he tried to actually glide a step or two.

"Well, I guess I'm not ready to give up on you, quite yet."

"As soon as we get back home, I'm calling the realtor. Maybe she can even start showing it before Josh and Katie's wedding."

"Okay. But just as long as you're sure, Randy. I want you to do this for you, not for me."

"I'd do anything for you, Josie. I love you so much."

"Then skate!" she laughed, as she let go of his arm.

And there went Randy, on his own, trying to balance himself, trying to stop, when his legs went out from under him and he hit the pavement, hard.

Trying not to laugh, Josie gracefully skated up to him and joined him on the ground.

"Ahh, are you okay? I'm sorry." And she kissed him on the cheek.

Randy looked at other skaters going around him and Josie and suddenly he wasn't embarrassed, at all. A super strength surged into him. He dipped his hand into his pant pocket and took out the engagement ring that Josie had returned to him. Then he struggled to get on one knee.

"Will you marry me, Josie? Please marry me."

A few skaters stopped to watch the romantic spectacle.

Tears came quickly to Josie's eyes. "I will. I will marry you."

And right there, in the middle of the skating path, he put the ring on her finger, then took her in his arms and passionately kissed her. Of course, just like in the movies, the crowd who had now gathered around them, started applauding.

She stared at the ring, then at Randy, then back at the ring. And then she planted a big one on his lips as the by-standers started clapping and hollering, again.

Now, embarrassed beyond belief, Randy tried to get up, but couldn't without Josie's help.

"C'mon, Randolph Four, let's go back to the hotel."

Amid congratulations from the smiling crowd, Josie and Randy shuffled away.

That night found the lovebirds sitting close to each other at a candle-lit table, having an after-dinner drink at a small restaurant next door to their Bed And Breakfast.

A rather drunk Randy was just staring at Josie. Just staring at her like a love-sick puppy.

"I... love... you, Josephine... Yes, I... do..."

"And I love you, Randolph Four." Josie was not nearly as drunk as he was.

"I love when you call me that. I love…
that… you are just… calling me… anything…"
And he burped, loudly.

"You are so cute when you're drunk. I've
never seen you drunk, before," she laughed.

"I don't get… drunk, very often, Missy…
but I think you got me… drunk, so I would lose
my in… ah… inha… bitions. Did you? Did you,
Miss Josephine?"

"Yeah! That's me. I did it." Josie
couldn't stop laughing.

He nuzzled her neck. "Well… I like it!"

"Okay, but just don't make it an everyday
occurrence."

"Oh, no… Fear not, my pretty princess…
I am not my father… My dear old dad. I shall
be… straight like an… ah… an…"

"Arrow."

"Arrow. Right. Tomorrow, that's what I'll
be."

Randy then yawned, closed his eyes and
dropped his head, asleep, onto Josie's shoulder.

"Randy! Wake up. Wake up."

"I love you… Josie… Yes, I do…"

"And I love you. Now let's go back to the
hotel, okay?"

It took some doing to wake him enough to
be dragged out of the restaurant.

Cozy in their bed that night, Randy kept repeating and repeating, in his half drunken, half asleep state, "I love you, Josie. I love you. I love you..."

Josie smiled, kissed him on the cheek, cuddled closer to him and was out like a light.

CHAPTER FIFTEEN

DEAD AIM ON LOVE

Josh and Katie drove into the parking lot of the Winthrop Manor and immediately noticed that Randy's car wasn't there.

"Oh, no, where's Randy's car?" said an alarmed Katie.

"Didn't you tell him we were coming?"

Wanting to accommodate Katie's every whim, afraid the couple might change their mind about having their wedding there, Randy had told her to stop by anytime, day or night. But now they didn't know what to think. They certainly didn't want to look like they were trespassing on the property. On the other hand, so nervous were they about this meeting with the ghosts, it had never occurred to them how they could meet them with Randy around. What in hell would Randy think they were doing, anyway? And if all the ghosts actually materialized as Heather had done, would Randy be able to see them? And if he could, had Randy actually seen Heather and Katie talking under the weeping willow? No, it was obvious, they hadn't thought through this part of their grand scheme, very well.

"Let's go up to the house and be nonchalant, knock on the door and see what happens. Maybe Randy just took his car in to be serviced, or something," the trying very hard to be rational, Josh came up with. Of course, there was absolutely nothing rational about anything they were doing or thinking.

"But then, how did he get home? Wouldn't he have had to rent a car?" She sounded on the verge of hysteria. It was obvious the tension was getting to Katie.

"Katie, Katie, let's just go up to the house and play it by ear, okay? Now calm down." And Josh kissed her gently on the cheek.

They walked across the great lawn, feeling as though they were criminals, robbers, lawbreakers, trespassing on private property, out to do no good. For a few moments they completely forgot why they were there in the first place, to meet a bunch of ghosts.

After mounting the steps, they rang the front door bell and waited. Nothing. They rang the bell, again. Still nothing. They knocked on the door. Nothing, nothing, nothing, only silence. They called out Randy's name. Again, nothing.

It crossed through Katie's mind, that if Heather knew they were coming and Randy wasn't there, why didn't she show herself? And then it came to her, clear as a bell. She had made this whole thing up in her mind. There was no Heather. There were no ghosts. There was no meeting. Was she living a dream? Had she manufactured all this in her head? After checking out the Winthrop Manor for a possible wedding site on the internet and reading about its history and about some long dead folks who had married and died there, had she finally fallen asleep, exhausted and dreamed all this? Was the fact that she and Josh were standing at the front door of the Winthrop Manor, right this moment, still part of her dream?

"Pinch me," she said.

"Pinch you? Why?" asked Josh.

"Because I think I'm sleeping and having a dream and I want you to wake me up, that's why!"

Josh put his arm around her. "You're not dreaming, Katie. C'mon, let's look around the place."

"See, I knew you'd say that! That's because I'm writing my own dream. And now we're going to walk around and the ghosts are going to come out and we're going to help them and everyone is going to live happily ever after. Right?"

"That's right, Honey. Now come on." And Josh led her around the Manor to the huge back yard.

The property seemed to go on for miles. A huge pool. A tennis court. A large fountain where ceramic angels seemed to be dancing in the fountain's water.

The two mounted the back porch steps. The veranda looked like it was out of a Southern plantation, with it's white rattan furniture, a large swing and couches with colorful soft pillows plumped up on them. Huge baskets with ferns and flowers hung from the white latticed over-hang. Seeing it, having a soft Southern drawl flashed through Katie's mind, along with the sudden desire to have a Mint Julep. In the times she had come to the Manor, for some reason, she had never ventured back here. Of course, perhaps that was all part of her dream.

Josh went up to the back door and knocked. Nothing, again.

"Maybe we should go back to the willow, Katie. Maybe that's where Heather is waiting for us."

"Okay," said Katie in her dream-like state.

He took her by the hand and started to lead her down the porch steps.

Just then, seemingly out of nowhere, Heather materialized right in front of them. So surprised was Josh, he tripped backwards.

"See, you don't need a 'tripping' ghost," laughed Heather.

Not believing what he was seeing and truthfully secretly always thinking in the deepest recesses of his mind that Katie had made the whole thing up, Josh slowly walked closer to Heather and just stared at her.

For her part, Katie came out of her dream-like state and started talking very, very rapidly.

"Oh, Heather! Randy didn't answer the door and we couldn't get in and we thought the whole thing, our meeting with you was wrecked and… Oh, I'm so glad to see you and the truth is, I wasn't even sure any of this was really real, but wow, here you are!"

Josh was still in a semi-paralyzed state. "Ah, Katie, Honey, calm down…"

"Oh, Heather, this is Josh! Josh, this is Heather!" Katie was bubbling over with disbelief and belief at the same time. And she repeated, "We knocked on all the doors, but…"

"Katie… we don't use doors," laughed Heather.

"Oh, right. Right…" And Katie finally took a deep, deep breath.

Josh continued to just stare at the ghost, now wondering if he was the one who was dreaming.

"Hi, Josh," said Heather, smiling shyly.

"You're really real," said the amazed Josh.

"What's real?" she asked.

"Maybe surreal is a better word. I'm sorry, I don't mean to stare."

Having gained, not all, but some of her composure back, Katie put on her therapist hat.

"Okay. Let's just pretend this is all just, you know, normal. So… where are the others? We can't wait to meet them!"

"They'll be here. Let's sit." Heather seemed much more composed than Katie and Josh.

"So where's Randy," asked Josh, as they all took seats.

"Oh, he went away for a few days with his girlfriend. They've been having some relationship issues. I know, because I was listening when you talked to him the other day, Katie. Maybe he took your advice."

"Oh, good. This is perfect, then! Now we won't have to pretend to be looking around again planning our wedding."

At that very moment, without any warning, the other five ghosts fully materialized. Jimmy, Jack and Randolph One were sitting on one of the rattan couches, Susanna and Mildred, on either side of Heather on the swing.

Seeing them, Josh and Katie almost had simultaneous heart attacks. It took everything in their power to try and remain calm, not to burst out hysterically laughing.

Heather made the introductions and to say everyone looked nervous was an understatement. Katie said, 'Hi,' and Josh said, 'Hey,' and the ghosts mumbled their own greetings. Katie mentioned how glad she was that they agreed to this meeting and Jack told her it wasn't as if they had come willingly. Jimmy admitted the whole thing was 'pretty trippy,' and Josh, trying to break the ice, told him he should definitely know about 'tripping.' It took a second for Jimmy to get it.

And then they sat and just stared at each other in that uncomfortable way that always happens at a first therapy session.

Oddly enough, it was Mildred who spoke up first. "What exactly do you expect to accomplish here, with us, Dears?"

"Honestly, Ma'am, we're not sure." admitted Josh.

"Well, we've been doing a lot of reading on the subject of death and ghosts and all and we just thought there must be a reason why you're still, well... here," added Katie.

"I'm here because I love it here! It's my home. I built it for my beloved Mildred." Of course this was Randolph One speaking.

Right on cue, Mildred rolled here eyes, something not missed by Josh and Katie.

Heather spoke to her ghost friends. "We've talked about it, remember? Maybe us still being here does have something to do with our relationships, our marriages"

"If I only still had one," whined Randolph One.

"Oh, will you get over it, already, Randolph One. You reap what you sow! Have I not told you that a million times?" Mildred was feeling feisty, although she had no idea why.

Katie immediately jumped upon this. "You sound angry, Mildred."

"Well, Dear, wouldn't you be if you had to hear that whining day in and day out?"

Then Jack put in his two cents. "So what, you two some kinds of Freud's or something?"

"Shut up, Jack. Maybe if you had thought more with your mind, instead of your gun, we'd still be alive!" Suddenly Susanna was seething.

"First of all, I didn't even get a chance to pull my gun outta my holster that night and second of all, do the math, Susanna, we would have been dead by now, anyway!" Jack spat.

Jimmy started counting on his fingers. "Hey, Heather, we would still be alive, Baby!"

"But we're not, are we, Jimmy? And all because of you!" Heather hit him with.

"Okay, folks, okay. It's obvious there's a whole bunch of anger and hostility between all of you. And it's a really good thing you're verbalizing it," Josh told them in the most professional manner he could muster.

"Are you kidding? That's all they do! Talk, talk, talk, talk and talk some more!" Jack said, with his own hostility showing.

"Yeah, how many times does a guy have to apologize, for crying out loud?" asked Jimmy.

"Until you guys start really hearing us!" yelled Susanna.

"Right on!" added Heather.

In a voice hardly above a whisper, Mildred said to Randolph One, "You never really ever listened to me."

"That's not true, Millie. Everything I did, I did for you, my Darling."

"Everything but listen to me," said a no longer feisty Mildred.

Again there was silence. And then Katie had an idea. She told them that she and Josh would talk with them, one couple at a time, so they could really try and find out the nitty-gritty of their problems and hopefully help them solve them, one way or another.

While Susanna and Mildred remained on the swing and Jack and Randolph One floated around the property, Katie and Josh talked with Heather and Jimmy at the weeping willow.

"I hate this tree, but I love it, too," started off Heather.

"Why?" asked Katie, already knowing the answer.

"Because we died here. But we were also married here and it was the most beautiful day. I thought we had our whole lives ahead of us and I was going to do so many great things."

"So was I, Heather! Why do you think you were the only one who lost their life? I was going to be a famous singer. I always thought I'd change world with my music, ya know?"

"You change the world by really *doing* something, like I was going to do. You change the world by getting involved in politics, like I was going to do and change the system!" Heather's face was getting red as she spoke.

"Well, creative people can change the world, too, Heather," said Katie. "Look at Sting. Or Bono."

"Who?" both Jimmy and Heather said at the same time.

"Never mind. The point is, we all have different dreams and different ways of trying to fulfill those dreams."

"But his weren't realistic, Katie."

"Yeah, well if the Beatles thought that way when they first got together, they'd still be in Liverpool!" Jimmy said angrily.

Josh didn't think this was the appropriate time to tell him that John and George were dead. But he added, "Jimmy does have a point."

"Thanks, Josh." Jimmy instantly decided he liked this Josh fellow.

"So what else was going on with the two of you?" asked Katie.

And so began the telling of how Heather believed that Jimmy just wanted her to stay at home and be barefoot and pregnant. And he saying how much he loved kids and wanted some of his own and how she didn't seem to want kids.

"And how did that make you feel, Jimmy?" asked Josh.

"Pissed. I don't know... like maybe she didn't love me enough to have my kids."

"Talk to her," Katie told Jimmy.

"Is that it, Heather? You didn't love me enough?"

"Of course I loved you, Jimmy. I just wasn't ready." And then she tried to explain it to Katie. "A bunch of our friends had kids and then split up. I had ambitions. And I didn't want to spend my days stoned like Jimmy and his friends and raising children in that kind of environment. I just wanted more."

"Tell him, Heather."

"I just wanted more, Jimmy."

"Yeah, well, I didn't want my old lady always being off somewhere, without me. I wanted us to be a team."

And the truth was beginning to surface.

Jimmy admitted how hurt he was that Heather didn't really, really believe in his talent. And Heather admitted that she did, but the thought of him not making it, getting so hurt if he didn't make it, would be too painful for her to watch.

"You can't always protect someone, Heather, no matter how much you want to," Josh told her.

"Don't you see, Heather," added Jimmy, "I would have rather died trying, then not try at all."

"Well, you did that, didn't you, Jimmy?" The anger was back in Heather's voice.

And now it was Jimmy who finally showed some anger. "Alright, already! I made a mistake! You keep acting like it only happened to you! My dreams died on that day, too!" And there was more than a hint of tears in Jimmy's eyes.

Heather saw this and felt a sympathy for him she hadn't felt before. She wanted to take him in her arms and comfort him. But she didn't.

Sensing a break-through, however small it might have been, Katie and Josh told them it was time to talk with the others, but perhaps they might stay under the willow tree and continue talking.

The next therapy session took place in the Grand Ballroom with Susanna and Jack.

Katie started. "So, what was it that first attracted you to each other?"

"Are you kidding? Look at her. She's a knock out!" Jack said. "Still is!"

Susanna looked a bit embarrassed.

"Well, you are! The first time I laid my eyes on your baby blues I knew you were the gal for me."

Jack told them how they both worked for a newspaper, how he was a lowly copy writer in the sports department and Susanna was the secretary to one of the editors.

"Yeah, Jack was a great writer. At that time, before all the bad stuff happened, he was in the middle of his first novel," Susanna told them.

"So, tell me Jack, how'd you get into the... illegal spirit profession?" asked Katie.

"Hey, a guy's gotta make a living, ya know? Then between some bad bets and borrowing money from the wrong people, well, one thing led to another. Then I met some people and eventually some opportunities arose I just couldn't refuse. But I never stopped writing."

"So if things started going your way, why didn't you take the money and run, get out of that life?" asked Josh.

"Hey, I was flying high, by then. Making such easy dough. It's hard to turn that down, ya know?"

"Yeah, Jack, easy money that got us killed," said Susanna holding on to her bitterness like it was 1928.

"I was gonna get out, Susanna! I was packing away enough dough so we could get outta town. Disappear and start a new life, somewhere else!"

"But I didn't want to go, anywhere, Jack! I was making a difference, moving up in the Party. My work was so important to me. We were changing people's lives. Unionizing the workers! I was helping to make the world a better place. But you had to go and ruin it. You ruined, everything!"

Jack just didn't get it. Didn't get it then, didn't get it now. "Why can't you understand that everything I did was for you?"

"Yeah, Jack, you got us killed for me!"

It took a lot to calm them both down, but eventually Josh and Katie got them talking, again.

"I hated your gangster friends! I hated your bootlegging! I hated what you did to our lives! My life, Jack!"

No, this wasn't going too well, thought the therapists.

But Jack went on to tell them how that night, the night of the party was going to be his last, how he had it all planned. He was going to stiff Winthrop One, take all the money from the night's party and all he had hidden and disappear where no one could find them.

"Wait a minute," said Josh, "You were going to stiff Randolph?"

"Long story, my friend, but he was getting kickbacks."

"Oh, right, I remember reading that, but there was something about no evidence to that fact," remembered Josh.

"Yeah, after he died and appeared one day, I reminded him. We thought it was sort of funny, us both ending up hanging around here. Turned out he later did some business with Benny The Blimp, then stiffed him royally. In fact, later he turned state's evidence and was the one who got the Blimp put away for life," laughed Jack.

Unfortunately, Susanna wasn't laughing. "And thanks, Jack, for including me in on all your elaborate plans for *my* life!"

"So, Susanna, why didn't you leave him?" asked Katie.

"I loved, him, Katie. I thought he'd change, that our lives would be different. His novel was so wonderful, I was sure it would get published, that he'd give up all that and..."

"And that you'd live happily ever after?"

"Yeah," Susanna said sadly. "Something like that."

"I loved you, too, Baby. And that's what I was going for. Ya gotta believe me," said Jack, showing for the first time some real emotion, some real sadness.

Susanna looked at her husband with just a whiff of sympathy.

Again, feeling they were making some progress, as they had with Heather and Jimmy, Katie and Josh left the two alone to continue talking, while they made their way up to the Master Bedroom and Randolph One and Mildred.

They found Randolph One sitting in his bed, while Mildred sat in her lounge chair by the window, the place she felt most comfortable. As always, it was the very spots that they had each drawn their last breath. Katie and Josh stood between the bed and the chair.

Immediately and surprising both Katie and Josh, Randolph One started the conversation.

"I built this house for my Millie."

'Well, I never liked it. Too big. Too many rooms," answered back Mildred.

This completely took Randolph One by surprised. "You never liked it? Never? Ever?"

"I rattled around this place for fifty years," said Mildred to Katie, never looking Randolph One in the eye.

"I came from old money. That's what you did for your wife. You built big. You bought big. You lived big,' said Randolph One proudly.

"Big, big, big!" Mildred almost heckled.

"Well, Millie, you certainly liked the big diamond ring I bought you. And your big car."

Mildred looked down at her left hand and twisted the beautiful, large, antique diamond ring she still wore on the ring finger of her left hand. "What did I know," Mildred said, sadly.

Katie went over and sat on the edge of the lounge chair. "What *did* you know, Mildred? If you didn't want all this, what did you want?" Katie's voice was gentle, soothing.

At first Mildred just thought, saying nothing.

"It was a different time for girls, back then. I didn't know I... *could* know, much of anything. Yes, he swept me away. But more than that, he swept my parents away. 'What a catch,' my father told me. I was so young, I didn't know my own mind. I knew I wanted children, lots of them, but we only had one son who lived. One I miscarried, very late and another died in childbirth. All sons."

"Oh, Mildred, I'm so sorry." Katie patted Mildred's leg, gently.

"I did what was expected of me. I was a good wife and a good mother. And I stuck by him through thick and thin."

"And then you left me, Millie." Randolph started to tear up.

Now Mildred showed some of her anger. "Only after you took up with that cheap starlet. And in your seventies, yet! Shame on you! Shame on you!"

Josh and Katie looked at each other in some surprise, but decided not to say anything.

"Mildred, you'd been ignoring me. Going to all your charity lunches and things. You never seemed to want to be with me. I was lonely and she cared for me."

"Stupid man! She didn't care for you, Randolph! She cared for your money. Only she didn't know there wasn't much of that left."

"It was a stupid fling, Millie. It meant nothing. Nothing." And Randolph One wiped his eyes with his striped pajama top.

"No, Randolph. It meant everything..." And Mildred turned away so no one would see her own tears.

And then their was silence, as the two old folks seemed to withdraw into their own cocoons of pain. It took a while of talking to them for Katie and Josh to get the conversation started again. They told them, whatever the outcome of any relationship, a couple must communicate with each other. Must be truthful. Must not let hostilities build up until the wall is so high, it cannot be overcome.

"He never saw me, Katie. He never saw the real me."

"Tell him, Mildred. Talk to him."

"You never saw me."

"What are you talking about? All I ever saw was you, my Darling." There was such a sad, pleading tone to Randolph's voice.

"No! You saw money schemes, you saw things! Always so busy scheming, buying…"

"For you, Millie. I did it all for you."

"But that's not what I wanted."

Silence again.

"What did you want, Mildred?" Katie asked, softly.

"I don't know… I don't know." And again the longest pause. "I just wanted you."

"But, Millie, I was always yours."

Anger boiled up in Mildred again. "No! Hers!"

"I was an old man. I was lonely. I didn't think you loved me, anymore."

Josh was so close to saying something to them, but Katie signaled with her eyes, not to.

Now tears were streaming down Mildred wrinkled cheeks. "But I did. I did love you."

Old Randolph One slowly got out of his bed and went to her, as Katie immediately got up and moved out of the way.

"We'll leave you two to talk a while, alright?"

They weren't listening, as Randolph sat down next to his love and took her hands in his, just as the old couple were hardly aware of the fact that Katie and Josh had tip-toed out of the room.

CHAPTER SIXTEEN

LOVE LOST LOVE FOUND

'… I am bound by that old promise;
What can break that golden chain?
Not even the words that you have spoken,
Or the sharpness of my pain;
Do you think, because you fail me
And draw back your hand today,
That from out of the heart I gave you
My strong love can fade away?
… Perhaps in some long twilight hour,
Like those we have known of old,
When past shadows gather round you,
And your present friends grow cold,
You may stretch your hands out towards me ---

Ah! You will, I know not when,
I shall nurse my love and keep it
Faithfully for you, till then.

Adelaide Anne Procter

Three different couples from three different decades who married and later died at the Winthrop Manor, floated through the days and months and years, stuck in their own now loveless, angry purgatory. Could it be that by finally looking each other in the eye, at last starting to communicate their individual pain to each other, they might be released to travel on their way, wherever that might be? That's certainly what Katie and Josh were hoping for.

The ghost's problems were universal. Any living couple could to attest to that. Everyone, male or female, alive, or in this case not alive, wanted something they didn't believe their mate was giving them, perhaps not capable of giving them. Understanding. Compassion. Attention. Sympathy. Empathy. Comfort.

After their one-on-one sessions with the couples and giving them some time to be alone, they all met back on the veranda, as the sun was beginning its decent in the west. The sweet smell from the honeysuckle vines permeated the area. For the first time in ages and ages, there seemed a calm between the three couples, as now they sat next to each other. Katie and Josh sat in chairs facing the six ghosts.

"I don't know, but after listening to all of you, it sounds to us that way down deep there is still love between you," Josh started things off with. "Maybe you didn't really know how to express it, but it sounds like you really did want what was best for each other, from your own point of view. I just feel you didn't always take your partner's views into consideration all the time."

"That's right," went on Katie. "Maybe you all felt you knew the answer for your mate, except, perhaps for Mildred. But Mildred, you came from a generation where wives were expected to be more like children, seen and not heard. The rest of you, well, your mates didn't always agree with your choices and then you turned away from each other in anger instead of really communicating your feelings and listening to theirs. And yes, of course, some of you died too soon, too young. I'd be angry, too. But did it ever occur to you why, in death, you've still remained together? Josh and I believe it was your choice. Do you all really want to stay here and argue, forever? Now we certainly don't know where you might go if you work out your relationship problems, but at least you wouldn't be fighting all the time, even if it were here that you stayed."

The four younger ghosts were quiet and thoughtful.

Josh took it from there. "Now all you seem to do, besides brawling with each other, is spending your time floating around here scaring poor, prospective brides and grooms."

"Only the ones who weren't meant to be together," said Susanna defensively.

"Oh! So you've taken it upon yourselves to make that assessment, have you?" said Katie. "Maybe because you're not happy, you don't want anyone else to be."

"No, really, Katie, some of these folks should not be married, trust me." Heather said seriously.

"Hey! We only did it because that's what the girls thought we should do!" said Jack, emphatically.

Josh let out a big laugh.

Katie gave Josh a slightly dirty look. "And you're all authorities on love and marriage, huh?" she continued.

The ghosts said nothing.

"Listen, you're powerless, over anyone but yourselves," Josh now said seriously.

"That's right. And you can't really protect anyone, either from harm or pain. It's a really hard lesson to learn, folks, but it's the truth," added Katie. "You've got to let go of all your anger, once and for all. Maybe you'll end up together... somewhere and maybe you won't, but now you're stuck. You've got to un-stick yourselves, one way or another. We don't know what else to tell you, but we just hope we've helped you begin to open the lines of communication with each other, a little."

In her mind Katie rolled her eyes around in her head. Jeez, she thought, I sound like something out of one of those psycho-babble books in the self-help department of a bookstore. What she would have loved to tell them is that yes, she had already become quite fond of all of them and hoped they found some happiness in... death, but please, please don't screw up our wedding, for crying out loud!

There was another thoughtful silence between the not living.

"Thank you, Katie. Thank you, Josh. I, for one, think this has been a good day for us. You've given us a lot to think about," said Heather, finally.

The others, even the men, smiled at the two therapists and nodded their heads. Katie and Josh rose. Katie wanted to hug all of them, but just didn't know if they were... huggable.

Heather and Jimmy started down the veranda steps, followed by Mildred, who took the stairs very slowly. Randolph One quickly went up to her, took her arm and gently led her down the steps. She didn't say anything to him, but on the other hand, she didn't smack him in the face, either. Katie and Josh thought this was progress. And then, right before their eyes, the ghosts turned into a foggy whiteness, then disappeared completely from their sight. As unnerving as this was to witness, the two took each other's hand, squeezed tightly and walked toward the parking area where their car was parked.

After they left, and invisible now, Susanna and Jack remained on the veranda's swing. Heather and Jimmy went toward the weeping willow and Mildred and Randolph One floated back toward the master bedroom. And the three couples talked into the evening. Yes, there were flashes of anger, tears and even a few laughs, as the three couples really talked, really communicated for the first time since their deaths.

Susanna and Jack swayed back and forth on the swing for hours. Finally, he put his arm around her shoulder, drew her closer and kissed her. And she kissed him back.

In the bedroom, Mildred and Randolph One sat on the edge of the bed, staring out into space. And then his hand creped closer to hers until he finally held it. She did not pull it away, as he hoped she wouldn't. Then he raised her hand to his lips and kissed it. Quite sweetly, they turned to each other, this very old couple, and lightly kissed on the lips.

At the old willow tree sat Heather and Jimmy, who was playing his guitar and singing to her. Mesmerized by his beautiful song, tears flowed from her eyes. When he was finished, she took the guitar from him, laid it down on the grass, then pushed him down next to it and kissed him with a great passion.

As a full moon rose high in the sky, twinkling stars dancing around it, Randy and Josie arrived home. Later, they were cuddled together in his bed in the guest house he called home. No, he could never bring himself to live in the Manor, itself. And the two fell asleep in each other's arms.

Cuddled together also, were Josh and Katie in their house. To say they were exhausted by the day's activity was an understatement.

"I think we did good, huh?" said Katie, before she dozed off into dreamland.

"Yeah, I think we did good," said Josh, sleepily.

"Do you think they all made up?"

"I don't know, Katie. Remember, even we're powerless. Maybe we gave them some tools to start them working out their problems."

"Oh, you, you sound just like a therapist," she laughed. And then she said, "Do you think it all really happened? Really?"

"I think it did."

They kissed each other and then within minutes were dead asleep.

CHAPTER SEVENTEEN

IS LOVE ALL YOU NEED?

Josie and Randy were working things out. After their weekend away they were closer than ever, with Josie staying at the Manor's guest house more than not. Randy, immediately, wanted her to give up her apartment, but she was hesitant. It wasn't that she didn't love him, she now just wanted to take things a tad slower, knowing the reality of him selling the Manor, might not have hit home with him, completely. To prove to her he was more than ready to leave the old and start anew, he couldn't seem to wait to put a giant 'For Sale' sign on the property. Josie felt this would be a mistake.

"The wedding you're giving is only a few months away, Honey. You're going to be so busy and you don't want realtors and prospective buyers tramping through the house all the time," she told him.

"Well, maybe I'll just tell Katie and Josh I'm selling and they'll have to find another place to get married! I just want to get rid of it and start a new life, with you!"

As much as that touched Josie's heart, somewhere inside of her, she just felt Randy hadn't thought through enough how the loss of his family's home would really affect him.

"I've waited this long, Randy. I can wait a couple of more months. Anyway, it will give us time to think about our own wedding, where we're going to live and all that good stuff!" And she hugged him tightly.

"Okay, you win, for now, but I'll need money from the sale for all that to happen," he said, nervousness creeping into his mind.

"Randy, I make a pretty darn good living. We'll be fine."

"I don't want to use your money, Josie! I'm the man!"

Suddenly Josie thought, perhaps women had not come a long way, baby. Was it just Randy's conservative views, that men should support their wives, that women shouldn't work... was it an ego thing, that to feel good about themselves, men still had to be in complete control... that men were better equipped to take care of one's family than women were? Whatever it was, Josie didn't like it. She had put herself through college, working at fast food joints and had supported herself ever since. She had started as a lowly secretary at an ad agency, working her way up in the company. Her dream was save up money, get enough personal clients and open her very own advertising agency. And she was so close to doing that. And he knew it.

"I think it's great, you having your own company, Josie," he told her. "But once we have children you'll be staying home."

Oops. Randy just lost a few points, as far as Josie was concerned.

"Randy, I love what I do. I can raise children and still work. Women do it all the time. It's the 21st century, for goodness sake!"

"Not my children! I had nannies throughout my childhood and hated it!"

After that, Josie stayed at her place, a little more often. She decided that Randy was quite emotional about, well, everything in his life at that moment and she would back off and take each day as it came. This could be worked out, she made herself believe. And she did love him. She did.

For Randy's part, he hadn't really thought about what in hell he would do after the Manor was sold. No matter how much he got for the place, he had so many debts to pay off. And then what would he do? What was he good at? What talents did he have? How would he make a living? Suddenly, Randolph Winthrop The Fourth became quite depressed. But one thing he was sure of and that was that he would not, could not live off his soon-to-be wife. But he did not share his deep concerns with Josie.

What Randy did do was haunt the halls that his great-grandfather had built, that he had taken such pains to revitalize. As much as he sometimes hated that big, old house and its past and what it represented, family-wise, he also felt such a strong, perhaps strange connection to it. Who really were these people he never got to meet? Who really was his own father, whom he hardly remembered? It was true, much as he sometimes tried to deny it, *Winthrop* was more than simply a name to him. He hated to admit it, but deep inside, he knew it was who he was.

Had Randolph Winthrop The First floated out of his bedroom more often and to places other than the Manor's basement, he would have realized that his great-grandson was really intending to sell the monument he had built for

216

his beloved Millie. And had he remembered that Heather had mentioned that to him, already, he would have been beyond appalled. But that's just not the way it is with ghosts. They don't always seem very interested in much of anything, unless, perhaps, it affected them, personally. And at that moment, some day in the future was a nebulous thought to him. All Randolph One cared about, was obsessed about, today, was getting his wife back into his arms, forever.

Oh yes, things had definitely improved since those human folks had had their little therapy day with the ghosts, but Mildred Winthrop was a stubborn woman.

"What did you want, Millie?" Randolph One asked his wife, as they laid on either side of their big marriage bed.

"I don't know. I didn't know I could really want anything," she admitted. "I was told what to do by my parents and then by you." And then she sighed, sadly. "I, I wanted my children who died to have lived. And then I felt like a failed you when they didn't, like I had done something wrong to have that happen."

"No, no, no, my Dear. You never failed me. I failed you. Now I see that I didn't really know what was important. I thought if I gave you diamonds and furs, then you'd be happy, that I could take all your sadness away. That's what a man was supposed to do. That's what I was taught. And then their wives were supposed to be satisfied. Happy. But you weren't, were you?"

"What is happiness, Randolph One?"

"You are my happiness," he said, as he took her age-spotted hand in his.

And they talked in the next days more than they had in all the years of their marriage. Really talked. And even though Mildred never quite forgave him for his indiscretion, she almost began to understand what had driven him to do it. And now, after all these years, what did it really matter? They were both long dead and it was time to come to terms with their life, such as it was… or rather, their ghostly present.

Susanna and Jack spent a lot of time talking, also. But as was Mildred, Susanna was a stubborn woman, too. A hanger-on of old wounds, quite literally in her case.

"You know, Jack," she said to him one day, sitting at the long wood bar in the Grand Ballroom, "sometimes I still feel the pain of Benny The Blimp's bullets as they tore through my gut."

"Let it go, already, Susanna," Jack told her.

Although he admitted to her that right before he was taken out by the Blimp, his life passed before his eyes and he regretted so much.

He regretted getting into the bootlegging business, he regretted thinking that making all that illegal money would be the answer to his future, their future.

"The only thing I didn't regret, as the blood was pouring out of my body, seeing you falling to the floor next to me, was loving you. If I could take back that day, if I could take back all the things I thought were important but weren't, I would, Susanna."

And her feelings softened towards her husband. "I wasn't perfect, either, Jack. I think I sometimes made the 'cause' more important than you."

"Truthfully, I was jealous of your passion for changing the world, for wanting to make a difference. I was jealous of your comrades, you spent so much time with. I wanted to give you things they couldn't, even though I knew you never had an interest in all the money I was making. But to me, money was freedom, so I could hide away and just write and write. And just be with you."

"Did we waste our lives, Jack?"

"I don't know," he answered, a frog now caught in his throat.

"I wanted to make the world a better place and really, so did you, with your writing and neither of us did, did we? Is that what life is supposed to be, just struggling to do something you think is right, for one reason or another, but never succeeding?"

"But we found each other, Susanna and even though it didn't end up the way either of us would have liked, we found each other and we loved."

"We did," she said. "We did, but then we wasted so much of our time together, fighting, angry at each other. Is that the lesson, here?"

"Well, if it is, what kind of crap is it to learn it after we're dead?"

And they looked at each other, with a love renewed. He asked for her hand, then walked her into the middle of the great room and to music in their heads, they held each other close and danced.

A light spring rain fell on the weeping willow, but Heather and Jimmy didn't notice. Unlike humans, ghosts aren't obsessed about the weather. Leaning back on the old tree, Jimmy's guitar nearby, they, too, spent much time talking. And as with the other women ghosts, it was hard for Heather to let go of the past. Considering she was the only one of the ghosts who peeked around the Manor, especially Randy's office, she was more aware of the world, as it was now. And she certainly didn't like the direction it had gone in. Had she lived, might she have become a Congresswoman, a Senator, maybe even the country's first woman president? Might she have been the one to end discrimination of all kinds, wars and hate?

"Dream on, Heather," an almost laughing Jimmy said.

"Don't laugh at me, Jimmy! It just takes a lot of individual people working together to change the world."

"My songs could have helped. Rallied the masses."

"Dream on, Jimmy."

"Well, maybe had we had children and they believed the way we did and then they had children, we could have bred generations who believed the way we did, like the Kennedy family," he told her.

"And most of them died young, just like we did, before they could really do anything of real consequence. I think it's true, Jimmy, the good do die young. Why is that?"

"I don't know," he said with remorse in his voice. "I'm so sorry I got mad that day, Heather. I just felt… I don't know what I felt or was thinking. I'm so sorry."

"Water under the bridge, now, I guess, huh?" she said.

"I guess. But I just want you to know that if we stay here or if we go, I don't know, somewhere else, I love you. I still love you and I never, ever meant for that to happen."

She leaned into his arms. "I know, Jimmy. I know."

And they kissed, as the rain came down a little harder.

"Will you sing me a song?" she asked him.

He picked up his guitar and began to sing a love song he had written for her about how in the end, all you really need in this life is love.

At the same time, things were unfortunately getting a little prickly between the two soon-to-be married therapists. Josh wanted salsa music at the wedding, while Katie wanted oldies but goodies. He preferred chicken for the luncheon entrée, while she was more inclined to go with seafood. He liked chocolate cake, while she thought they had already decided on lemon with vanilla icing. And for about seven hours they hardly spoke to each other. But being the psychologically adept folks that they were, they talked it through, realized what was really important in this life, made up and laughed about it.

Then they went back to the Manor, to finalize all the wedding details with Randy. As they drove up the winding driveway on a beautiful spring day, talk turned to the ghosts.

"Gosh, I hope they really worked out their differences," Katie said.

"Well, I think we did everything we could do. And I think it was good to leave them alone a while."

The truth was, Katie had meant to go back to the Manor a few days after their marathon session to check in on them, but Josh had dissuaded her from doing so. They only argued about that for an hour and a half. As excited as she was to talk to Randy about their up-coming nuptials, she couldn't wait to see if they had succeeded in helping the ghosts find peace with each other, one way or another.

Randy was all business, as he listened to what Katie and Josh wanted, giving suggestions about the seating, the band, the flowers, the catering, the cake and on and on. Unlike other wedding sites, he would be taking care of everything for them. And both Katie and Josh were grateful for that.

"You're so good at what you do, Randy. And we wanted you to know how much confidence we have in you. I think you were born to do this kind of work!" Katie told him.

Hearing that was rather bitter sweet for Randy, since he knew this would be his last wedding. Without Josie knowing it, he had talked to a realtor about selling the Manor, how much he might be able to get for it in the current economy and how long the realtor thought it might take to sell. The news on all fronts wasn't great... not as much as he had hoped and it might be on the market a good long time... but Randy was determined to rid himself of this monkey that was breaking his back.

After the meeting with Katie and Josh, Randy sat at his desk and started working off of all the notes he had taken. If this was going to be his final bow, it was going to be the most wonderful, most beautiful production of a wedding he had ever done.

Talking to himself out loud, he went over the plans. "Okay, lemon cake with vanilla icing. A band that plays oldies and salsa music. Chicken and seafood dishes..." And then he stopped himself. "Hm, maybe people do talk out loud to themselves," he said, thinking about seeing Katie on the lawn that day talking to *herself*. If he only knew.

Katie and Josh left the mansion in search of friendly ghosts. At the weeping willow they called out for Heather and Jimmy, but got no response. Around back at the veranda, they called out, albeit softly, for the rest of the ghosts.

Nothing. They didn't want to go into the Grand Ballroom or up to the master bedroom, because Randy was in the house and obviously, they couldn't be found looking for or talking to ghosts, in front of him.

But the ghosts didn't materialize.

"I wonder where they are?" said a worried Katie. "I hope they're okay. Maybe we should sneak down to the basement, where they said they hang out."

"Katie, we don't know where that is. Anyway, maybe they really worked out their problems and went… on to… wherever ghosts go when they work out their problems. I think we should consider our work a success and forget it."

"But we'll never see them, again. That's sad. I really liked them, especially the women. Especially Heather."

Josh laughed. "Oh, you'll get over it." But in his heart, Josh wondered what had happened to them, also.

"I just hope wherever they are, they're happy, now," said Katie.

"Me too, Honey. Me too."

Arms around each other, as they past by the weeping willow again, on their way to their car, Josh almost waited to be tripped, as a last joke from Jimmy and Katie looked up at the tree's branches, almost wanting one to float down on her, a last sign from Heather.

But there was only quiet, except for a bird chirping happily in the tree.

CHAPTER EIGHTEEN

DRESSES AND FLOWERS AND HAIR, OH MY!

Katie still hadn't picked out her wedding dress and time it was a wasting. She had already visited many bridal shops, but hadn't found the perfect dress, not by a long shot. By this point she was ready to walk down the rose-petaled aisle in a white T shirt and white pants.

Utterly abhorred by the very thought of it, and knowing her daughter might well do something like that, her mother, Bonnie, had almost shrieked in her face, "No! You can't do that! This is the biggest day of your life. Everything must be perfect! A long white lace dress with a long veil and a long train. You'll be the most beautiful bride that anyone has ever seen."

"Long, long, long! I don't like long, Mother!"

"But you have to stand out, Darling. Think of the pictures! A long white dress, on the green grass, although I really don't understand why you must be married outside. What if it's a windy day and your up-do comes down?"

"I'm thinking of leaving it down. Simple."

"Wedding's shouldn't be simple, Dear. Perhaps a lovely French Twist with curls framing your face."

"Too sixties."

"The French Twist never goes out of style, my Darling."

Katie wasn't in the mood to argue. "I'll think about it, Mom," she said in a placating manner.

As much as she loved her mother, Katie decided not to take her with her to this latest and hopefully last bridal shop she would ever visit.

And there, she was, hours later, standing on a platform in front of a three-way mirror in an elaborate long white dress of satin, with a very long train and borrowed white heels, Antoinette, the very French saleslady, with a very thick accent, had given her to wear for the trying on, hope you will buy, occasion.

Antoinette was attaching a very long veil to Katie's head with bobby pins.

"Ow!," cried out Katie, as one stuck her in her noggin.

"Ooh, I am so sorry, Madam," Antoinette apologized. "But your hair is quite thin."

Well, didn't that make Katie feel like a beautiful blushing bride. Once the veil was attached, Antoinette looked her over.

"Oui, oui, so lovely are you!" the saleslady gushed. "I think this is the one!"

As Katie gazed at her reflection, for a moment she pictured herself as Marie Antoinette, wife of Louis The Sixteenth, on the eve of the French Revolution, after hearing that crowds of poor peasants had complained there wasn't enough bread to go around, saying 'Let them eat cake!' Then she remembered from a French History class she had once taken in college, this was just a myth and the truth was it had been said a hundred years before by one Maria-Therese, the wife of Louis The Fourteenth, instead. And the truth of the matter was, the French quote had been lost in translation and really meant, 'Let them eat rich, expensive, funny-shaped, yellow, eggy buns.' She started to laugh out loud.

This Antoinette saleslady person thought Katie was laughing because she realized how beautiful she, indeed, did look and would buy the dress, the train and the veil, thus giving her such a large commission, she would be set in croissants for a very long time.

But her hopes were dashed when Katie regained her composure from laughing at her thoughts and said, "I don't know. It just seems a bit much for me."

"Merde!" Antoinette cursed under her breath.

Alone in the huge dressing room with wall to wall mirrors, Katie took one last look at herself, before undressing to try on one of the other many dresses that hung from a rack.

In an instant, who was to appear before her, than Heather, Susanna and Mildred. Katie almost fainted on the spot.

"No, definitely not you, Katie," said Heather, speaking of the dress.

"Much too fluffy. Poufy," said Susanna.

"I think you look like an angel, Katie, Dear. Like an angel in heaven," this, of course, from Mildred.

Katie was wide-eyed and speechless. Finally she managed, "What are you doing here? I thought you were gone... away. And... and how did you find me, and..."

"Funny thing." explained Heather, "Us girls..."

"Women, Heather, we're *women*, not girls…", this interruption surprisingly and amusingly from Mildred.

"Yes, Mildred, us *women* were just sitting around talking about you and how much you and Josh helped us all and thinking about your wedding and everything and then, whoosh, here we are."

"Wow," was all Katie could come up with.

"We didn't even know we could do this. We didn't know all this time that we could, you know, go places!" Susanna told her, excitement in her voice.

"Had I have known, I would have gone to Venice. I always wanted to see Venice," added Mildred, dreamily.

"I would have gone to the Left Bank in Paris," said Susanna. "All those writers and artists who lived there…"

"I don't know where I would have gone. Maybe Tibet. Or India. You know, to help the downtrodden, the poor," said Heather.

"Are you okay, Dear," this was from Antoinette, checking in on her customer through the closed door.

"Yes. Yes. I'm just going to try on some of these other dresses, if that's okay," Katie called back to her. "I'll let you know if I need you."

"Oui, Madam. I am here for you. Oui."

Now Katie kept her voice to a very low whisper. "I can't believe you're here! So, is everything okay?"

The ghosts filled her in on how they were now really communicating with their spouses and how they were coming to terms with their deaths and trying to over-come any negative feelings they had had bottled up inside of them all those decades.

"That's great! But you're still... here," Katie said.

"And maybe we always will be, but it's okay, now. It really is, all because of you and Josh," Heather told her.

"Okay, onto the next dress! You have a wedding to worry about now, Katie, not us," Susanna told her, with conviction in her voice.

The next dress she tried on was a slinky little barely there silk number.

"Oh, yes," gushed Susanna. "I couldn't get away with it, but you look fabulous!"

"Oh my no! You want a little mystery, Dear. This leaves nothing to the imagination. Don't you know imagination is... sexy?" giggled a now lighthearted, yet a slightly embarrassed by her own thoughts, Mildred.

Katie laughed, out loud, then put her hand over her mouth, hoping Antoinette didn't hear her.

Heather just shook her head, 'no.'

The next dress Katie stepped into was a simple lace number, right out of the 70's.

"Perfect!" It's perfect! Why wasn't this Vera Wang person around in my day?" Heather mused, reading the designer tag hanging from the side of the dress.

"Not bad. But you can do better," commented Susanna.

"That's not a wedding gown, Dear. Where's the tulle? Where are the layers? The train. No, no, it's all wrong. All wrong to be married in," added Mildred.

By now Katie was tired, completely confused and frustrated. "I'm never going to find the right dress for me!" she said in a loud voice.

Just then Katie's mother burst into the dressing room, stared right through the ghosts and looked at her daughter.

"Mom! What are you doing here?"

Ignoring her question, Bonnie eyed her daughter up and down. "That's pretty, but not you... of course, unless you love it, Dear"

Mildred agreed with an adamant 'no' shake of her head. Heather shook her head, 'yes.' Susanna shrugged.

First panicked, then realizing her ghost women couldn't be seen by anyone except her, she took a deep breath and said, "I don't know, Mom. I haven't really liked anything, so far."

"Not to worry. Mother's here, now. I'll help you find the perfect dress."

Was that jealousy in the ghost's eyes that Katie noticed. Yes, it was, which made Katie smile.

Days later, while the dress problem had yet to be settled, next on Katie's agenda were the flowers. Walking through the long aisles of the flower mart, downtown, Katie was slightly dizzy by all the fragrances filling her nostrils. She stopped and turned back to the hundreds of cans of roses, when who was she to see, but Mildred, Susanna and Heather. This time, not only wasn't she surprised, she was comforted by their presence.

"Yes, roses, my Dear. The place must be filled with roses. They're the flower of love, you know." And then Mildred closed her eyes, remembering her own wedding. "At my wedding to Randolph One we had roses and roses and more roses. Reds and pinks and white ones. What a glorious sight they were. The flower of love."

Katie warmly looked at the old woman and knew in her heart that Mildred still was in love with Randolph and she hoped she had expressed those feelings to him.

They continued down the aisle.

"Oh, look!" exclaimed Susanna. "Lilies! I carried a bouquet of lilies when I was married. White lilies and baby's breath."

"But remember, Susanna, I gave you a red rose to hold, also, when you and Jack married at the Manor?"

"Yes. Yes. I remember," said Susanna. And she leaned down and kissed Mildred on her cheek.

Then Heather saw glass vases filled with daisies. "Lilies are too fancy. Daisies would be perfect, Katie. And a wreath of them in your hair. Perfect and simple.

"Roses!"

"Lilies!"

"Daisies!"

Katie looked at all three of them. "Maybe I'll just carry a bunch of weeds! Or better yet, how 'bout Venus Fly Traps?"

"Oh, Katie, you're so silly. Roses!" And Mildred dragged her back to see her flower of choice.

With no flowers set in stone and no dress yet picked, Katie found herself sitting in the chair of one of the top hairdressers in Beverly Hills, George, of the famous George Salon. Her mother had made the appointment for her as a trial run of different styles Katie might want her hair to look like.

Hovering over her were the very opinionated ghost women.

"A short, straight bob," insisted Susanna.

"A nice conservative bun, with wisps of hair coming out of your veil, Dear," suggested Mildred.

"Long and straight with some braids in the front," Heather told Katie.

Of course, Katie could say nothing to her ghostly friends, who quite frankly were driving her a little nuts, by now, although she knew they were doing it out of love.

After George had slaved for hours, giving Katie every conceivable style known to woman: ups, downs, twists, knots, half up-half down, elaborate braids coming out of her head, part in the middle, part on the side, no part, four parts, low ponytail, high ponytail and on and on, Katie still wasn't happy.

"Maybe I'll just wear a wig," she said blandly.

By the end of the long appointment, the ghosts had almost fallen asleep. George was ready for a long nap, also.

On her way home, with the ghosts sitting in the backseat of her car, Katie told them, "Ya know what, I really thank you guys for all your help with my hair, my dress, the flowers, but I'm now going to just think about everything, alone, okay?"

In her rear-view mirror, Katie saw the ghosts nod. But they didn't look all that happy.

"C'mon, guys, it's nothing personal, okay? I loved and appreciated all of your suggestions with everything, but I have to pick what's right for me."

"Of course, Katie. It's your special day," said Susanna

"We just wanted to help you anyway we could, that's all," added Heather.

"And you have. You have."

"Roses!" piped in Mildred. And they all laughed.

"So, can I drop you anywhere," asked Katie, actually forgetting for a moment she was talking to ghosts.

"Naw. We need the exercise and the fresh air will do us good. We'll just float home," Heather said, without an inkling of sarcasm in her voice.

"We love you, Katie," Susanna told her.

"I love you all, too," Katie told them, looking into her rear-view mirror, again. But they were gone.

At a stop light, Katie looked into the mirror, again and fiddled with her hair. "Hm, maybe I could braid the front, bob the sides and have a little bun in the back." And then she laughed and drove off toward home.

CHAPTER NINETEEN

OH HAPPY DAY

It was finally June... of course, the ultimate month for a wedding. It was Josh and Katie's long anticipated day of matrimony, where they would promise to love, honor, but not necessarily obey each other, until death do they part. Considering the history of the Winthrop Manor, they certainly hoped that wouldn't happen any time soon. The night before, they had joked how they would think twice before going back to the Manor after being married there, possibly to have the bad luck to die in, say, an earthquake on that unfortunate day and spend the rest of eternity haunting those hallowed halls, since what would be the chance of another couple of therapists wanting to marry there, figuring out that the now tripping, slapping, swaying, branch-dropping, window slamming, goosing ghosts, Katie and Josh, hadn't worked out their marital problems in life, try to help them so they could finally be released from their purgatory and live happily ever after in some great beyond. Whew!!!

"That's a creepy thought, huh?" laughed Josh.

"Well, just to be on the safe side, let's not ever go there, again," laughed Katie.

"But we're spending our wedding night there. We'll already be married. What if an earthquake really happens tomorrow in the middle of the night and demolishes the Manor and we die," said Josh, now somewhat concerned.

"Don't worry, Honey. By tomorrow night, we won't have had time to have problems in our marriage!" Katie told him.

"That's true."

"See? All better!" laughed Katie, again. And she kissed him.

Katie had finally found the perfect dress at a vintage store, she sometimes frequented, to be wed in. She had found the perfect flowers to decorate the tables in the Grand Ballroom and to hold, as she walked down the petaled path to meet her soon-to-be husband. She had also decided how she wanted her hair and she came to all those decisions by herself, with no ghosts and no mother by her side trying to manipulate her brain. And now she couldn't wait.

The day dawned bright, with only a hint of a breeze. The Manor was a flurry of activity, with Randy running around like a chicken with his head cut off, making sure everything was perfect, the food, the chairs, the band, everything. And Josie was right by his side, helping out, trying to calm her poor man down. Their relationship was again on solid ground and working as a team on this wedding was inspiring to both of them.

The last thing to be done was having some workers roll out the white cloth aisle down the lawn, near to the weeping willow, where Katie and Josh would say their vows under a beautifully flowered-covered gazebo.

"Oh, Honey, everything looks so beautiful. You did good!," Josie told Randy.

"You really think?" said a very nervous Randy.

"I think," she assured him, then kissed him on the lips. "I'm going to go check on the bride and see if she needs anything." And she went toward the Manor, as Randy looked around the wedding area, moving a few of the guest chairs an inch here or there. Perfect.

Katie had told her mother and bridesmaids that she just wanted some time alone before her big moment. The bridesmaids understood and didn't take it personally. Bonnie, not quite so much and lingered after her friends left.

"But Katie, I'm your mother, for goodness sake! I should be here with you."

"Just a little while, Mom. I just want to think, take it all in, alone, okay?"

"But you'll call me if you need me, won't you?"

"I will, Mom. And I love you," Katie told her.

"You look beautiful, Honey, even with those curlers in your hair."

"Thanks, Mom."

Bonnie kissed her daughter on the cheek and reluctantly left the room. Katie took in a deep breath.

A few minutes later, the bedroom door opened, a crack.

"Hi, Katie, I'm not bothering you, am I?"

"Of course not, Josie." Katie was just relieved it was not her mother, back again.

Katie had only met Randy's love once before, when she and Josh had stopped by to make some final wedding arrangements. Josie entered the master bedroom to find Katie sitting in front of the vanity in a bathrobe, putting the finishing touches of make-up on her face.

"I just wanted to know if you wanted any last minute anything?"

"Oh, no thanks. I think I have everything under control here. But thanks."

"It looks so beautiful down there. When Randy and I get married, could I borrow some of your wedding ideas?"

Katie smiled warmly at her. "Of course. Is it going to be soon?"

"Truthfully, I wasn't sure it was ever going to happen, but Randy's really changed, lately. Besides today, since he's obviously a nervous wreck, he just seems like he's enjoying life, everything, more than he used to. Things are good."

Katie smiled at her. "I'm so glad to hear that, I really am."

"Well, I'll leave you alone to get ready, but call me if you need anything. Your guests should be arriving soon, so… have a happy, happy day."

"Thanks, Josie."

Once Josie was gone, Heather, Susanna and Mildred immediately materialize.

"I thought they all would never leave! We have things to do, here!" said Susanna. And she started taking the rollers out of Katie's hair.

"Oh, Katie, you're going to look so beautiful," said Heather.

"Thanks, Heather."

"Now, Katie, it's your wedding, Dear. Have you forgotten you must have something old, something new, something borrowed and something blue?"

"Oh, no! I did forget. Does that mean bad luck?" Katie said seriously, looking around, as if all those things would suddenly materialize before her, also. "Oh, wait! My dress is new! ... Oh, no, it's not a new dress, at all. My shoes, my shoes are new!"

"One down, three to go," Heather laughed.

"This isn't funny, Heather!" scolded Katie.

Then Mildred handed Katie a very old looking, small jewelry box.

"What's this?" asked Katie.

"Open it, Dear, it's for you," said Mildred lovingly.

Inside the box was the most beautiful antique heart necklace.

"Oh, Mildred, I don't know what to say. It's so beautiful."

Mildred took it out of the box and put it around Katie's neck.

"Randolph One gave it to me the day we were married. It's my special gift to you, my Dear. I won't be needing it, now."

With tears in her eyes, Katie gave Mildred the biggest hug.

"Two down, two to go!" said Heather.

Susanna then raised her skirt and rolled down one of her stockings which was being securely held to her leg by an old fashioned black garter.

"This is your 'borrowed,' Katie. I know it's not sexy, but it was all I could come up with. But I'm afraid I'll need it back later, okay? Otherwise I'll look pretty stupid dancing at your reception with one stocking rolled down to my ankle."

Katie rolled it up her leg. "Thank you, Susanna, I love it." And they hugged, also.

"One more left, bride! I have something blue for you," said Heather as she took off her pinky finger a thin turquoise band, which she placed on Katie's right hand pinky finger. It fit perfectly. "I know it's not blue, blue, but…"

"It's perfect, Heather. It's all so perfect." And Katie began to cry as she hugged Heather. 'I don't know how to thank all of you."

"Thank us? We thank you, Katie. You've given us so much. You've made our death, almost worthwhile," said a now teary Heather.

And they all laughed, not a 'ha-ha' laugh, to be sure, but rather a sweet and sentimental laugh and then they all gathered 'round for a warm group embrace. Even with her friends, even with her family, Katie thought she had never felt such warmth from others as she did at that moment, from three dead women.

"Well! Let's get you dressed. And look at your make-up, it's all smeared now, Dear. You don't want to be late for your own wedding, do you?" asked Mildred. "Now that would be bad luck."

In the meantime, in one of the other Manor bedrooms, Josh was getting ready, himself. He didn't think he'd be that nervous, but he was, as he paced the floor, wearing tuxedo pants and a starched white shirt. Hanging on the closet door was his jacket and tie. He was hoping the male ghosts might show up, but thus far, they were nowhere, at least that he was aware of.

There was a knock at the door. Josh knew that wasn't his ghost friends, since they didn't need door to enter, anywhere.

"Come in."

Randy entered the room, looking more nervous than Josh.

"So, Josh, ready for your big day?

"Oh, yeah!. A little nervous, but I can't wait. Hey, thanks, man, the place looks amazing. You've done a great job for us."

"Well, you're my swan song, Josh, so I really wanted to do it up for you and Katie."

"Swan song? What'd you mean?" asked Josh.

"Well, I'm selling the Winthrop Manor." It was hard for Randy to actually say those words out loud.

"Selling it? You're kidding. Why?" said a completely surprised Josh.

"Well, truthfully, I just can't afford it, anymore. Yours is the first wedding I've booked in months and months. This place is a dinosaur. So many couples have looked at it, but in the end, no one wanted to be married here. It's almost like they're scared of, I don't know, maybe having their wedding at a place like this."

Josh knew exactly what those couples were scared of, but he certainly wasn't going to share that information with Randy.

"Well, maybe our wedding will turn your luck around. There's certainly nothing to be scared of here."

"No, Josh, the truth is, I've run out of money. It would take a miracle for me to be able to keep this place. And I really don't believe in miracles." Randy looked really depressed, now.

"And Josie and I are going to get married and everything, so I just need a clean start in life."

"But it's been in your family for a hundred years."

"I know. If my great-grandfather knew, he'd turn over in his grave. But it's become a curse to me. I almost lost Josie because of my obsession with it. And it was Katie who really turned my head around. She really made me come to my senses about what's important in this life. And it's not this old house."

"Wow," was the only thing Josh could come up with. Then, after a moment, "Well, I'm just glad it was still here for us."

"Yeah… well, I'm going to make one more quick check of everything. Your guests should be starting to arrive soon and I want to be there to greet them. Good luck, Josh."

"Yeah, you too…"

Randy left the room, but he looked like a beaten man. Josh turned around to get his jacket, when he was suddenly face to face with Randolph One. Behind him stood Jimmy and Jack.

"He's going to sell my home!? That little ingrate! And because of Katie!?" Randolph One bellowed. "Wait a minute! Now I remember Heather telling me that boob was thinking of selling my house, but… then I forgot. How could I forget something like that?"

"Calm down, Randolph One. And you can't blame Katie. She was just helping him with some personal relationship problems he and his girlfriend were having, just like we helped all of you."

"Some help!" Angry smoke seemed to be coming out of Randolph One's ears.

"And why didn't you know, before, for crying out loud?" questioned Josh. "I mean, you're here all day and all night! How could you not have known? Didn't you see or hear what was going on?"

"Hey! I'm a ghost! What do I know? Okay, so I wasn't watching. All these years, Randolph Four hasn't been... part of my... death. Ingrates, all of them! My son, my grandson and now my great-grandson. I should have been paying better attention. Just like I should have been paying better attention to Mildred. I failed them all in life and in death."

"This sucks big time," said Jimmy

"Yeah, he's selling our home!" Jack complained.

"My home! My home!" yelled Randolph One.

"Sorry, One. You know what I meant," said Jack.

"I can't let him do that! I won't!" Randolph One was mad as hell and he wasn't going to take it anymore!

"Let's talk about it later, okay, guys? Maybe I can help. I'll talk to Randy. But in the meantime, I gotta meet my beautiful bride down there. I'm really sorry, Randolph One," Josh told him, but Randolph One wasn't listening. A second later he disappeared in a white puffy huff.

"This sucks big time," repeated Jimmy.

"Yeah," said Jack.

As Josh turned away to grab his jacket and tie, the two remaining ghosts disappeared, also.

Down on the lawn the guests were seated and a string quartet played classical music. The wedding was about to begin, as Josh stood under the flowered gazebo next to a woman judge. Standing on either side were four bridesmaids and four groomsman. Standing next to Josh were Jimmy and Jack, of course, seen only to the wedding couple. In the back, behind the chairs stood Randy and Josie, holding hands.

The music changed to 'Here Comes The Bride,' as the beautiful Katie, flanked by her parents, started her walk down the white cloth aisle, strewn with red and pink rose petals, towards Josh and her new life. Her vintage white dress was simple and flowing, her hair, topped by a flowered wreath was lightly curled. Her wedding bouquet was made of roses, lilies, daisies and baby's breath. Behind her walked Heather, Susanna and Mildred.

Not seeing Randolph One with the other male ghosts distressed Mildred, terribly. Where could he be, on this, such an important occasion, she thought. Then, just as she was thinking she would never speak to him again and all their therapy and recent communication was for naught, Randolph One materialized next to Jack. Immediately they locked eyes, as Randolph One blew a kiss to his beloved. Mildred blushed, as only a ghost could blush.

With Katie's parents seated in the front row, and Josh reaching out his hand for his own beloved, the ceremony began. The judge talked about love and marriage and commitment, then told the happily gathered family and friends that Katie and Josh wanted to say their own personal vows to each other.

Josh spoke first. "Katie, my Darling, I promise that throughout our life together, I will listen to you, respect you and always love you. You are my love and my life and today you have made me the happiest living man on this earth."

Then it was Katie's turn. "And I will listen to you, respect and always love you, too. Not only throughout our life together on this earth, but through all of eternity, even when our bodies cease to exist, because I believe, I know, that our love for each other, real love, will go on forever and ever, until the end of time, itself..."

There wasn't a dry eye among the living or the dead.

'I do's' were said and rings exchanged and then the grand finale, the first kiss being husband and wife. Then applause and cheering filled the Manor's lawn, as the couple went back up the aisle smiling and laughing at all their well-wishers. Behind them the ghost couples reached for their partner's hands and followed the newlyweds back toward the Manor, the Grand Ballroom and the newly married couple's first dance together.

CHAPTER TWENTY

<u>ONE LAST DANCE</u>

At the reception, dinner was delish and everyone was in a festive mood. Toasts were made as the lovebirds sat at the edge of the dance floor at their own little table. Josh took Katie in his arms for the first dance. The couple had had many discussions of what that first dance would be. Josh thought the Beatles, 'Will You Still Love Me When I'm Sixty-Four' would be fun. Katie nixed that one. She liked Lionel Richie's, 'Hello,' but Josh said 'goodbye' to that idea. There was always, 'Love, Will Keep Us Together,' but they both shook their heads in the negative on that one. Finally they came together on Nat King Cole's, 'When I Fall In Love, It Will Be Forever.' When the musical strains began it brought out 'ahh's,' from the guests and more teary eyes, as Josh held his bride close and kissed her as he twirled her around, then close to him.

Later, Katie had a surprise for the ghosts. When the band played a Charleston, Jack and Susanna did such a mean one, her beret almost fell off her bobbed-haired head. When 'Let The Sun Shine,' from 'Hair' filled the Grand Ballroom, Heather and Jimmy hippy love danced all over the place. And when the Viennese Waltz began, Randolph One, in his striped pajamas and Mildred could have won a dance competition, as he glided her gracefully around the floor. The guests thoroughly enjoyed dancing to all this musical nostalgia, also, obviously never knowing why the bride and groom had picked these songs for the band to play. Katie, especially, got teary-eyed, watching her dead friends dancing the night away.

Out of the huge Ballroom windows, the sun was beginning its decent behind the western hills of Los Angeles and the June fog began to roll in from the ocean. A wind started blowing through the Hollywood Hills, as tired wedding guests finally walked past the weeping willow tree toward the parking area and their cars. The night was ending for them, as a new life was beginning for Katie and Josh.

After the last hug and kiss from friends and family and thanking Randy again and again for giving them such an extraordinary wedding, an exhausted, but utterly ecstatic Josh and Katie retired to the Master Bedroom. They plopped down on the huge, canopied bed for a moment, lost in their own happy thoughts.

"Wow!" laughed Katie.

"Wow!" laughed Josh.

"We did it!"

"We sure did," said Josh, as he tackled her, kissing her all over her face. Then just as he started to take off her wedding dress, he heard someone clear their throat. They both popped up to see Randolph One standing at the foot of the bed.

"No, no, no, Randolph One. This room is off limits, now," said a tad annoyed Josh.

They had never thought of the fact that their ghosts might, could, would float into the privacy of their wedding night! What to do? What to do? If they told them that was not acceptable behavior, would the ghosts even listen? And how would they even know if they were being watched, spied on?

Katie leaned close to Josh, whispering in his ear, "Maybe we should just leave and get a hotel."

"Let's see what he wants," Josh whispered back.

"I can hear you!" said Randolph One. "I'm no pervert, peeping Tom, I just want to talk with you a moment, Josh."

"Now?! Can't it wait, One? This is really an inopportune time."

"No!" Randolph One angrily stated. "I don't have much time." Then his voice softened. "Everything is at stake, Josh. Please. Please, it will just take a minute." The old man was holding an old mid-sized valise close to him.

Something in his voice told both Josh and Katie that the old man needed to be tended to. Josh reluctantly got off the bed and followed the old man out of the bedroom and into the hallway.

"Now, what's so important?" Josh asked.

"You got to do me a favor," he said desperately. "You got to take this valise down to Randolph Four!"

"Okay, I'll do it in the morning."

"No!" Randolph One cried out. "Now! Now!"

"Calm down, please. Why now? What's in it?"

'It's for my great-grandson to open. No

questions, okay? Just please do it for me. I'll never ask you for another thing." He sounded half hysterical.

"Okay, okay. I'll do it right now."

So very relieved, Randolph One handed the old suitcase to Josh.

"Will you just go and tell Katie I'll be right back?"

Randolph One nodded and started going back into the bedroom.

"Wait," called out Josh. "What should I tell him?"

"Just tell him you found it somewhere... In the bedroom you were dressing in. Something. Anything."

Josh nodded and went on his way.

In Randy's office, Josie was sitting on his lap, kissing him.

"Wasn't that the most beautiful wedding, Randy? And didn't you love their personal vows?"

"Yeah. We should write our own vows, too. I love you, Josie."

"But are you sad? You can tell me the truth."

"Truth? I guess I do have mixed feelings about selling this old place, but I know I'm doing the right thing," he said.

And Josie saw his sadness and starting kissing him, again. Just then Josh entered the room, without knocking. Seeing them kissing, he almost went back out of the room. But Randy saw him.

"Hey, Josh. What are you doing here? Everything's okay, isn't it," Randy asked.

"Oh, yeah, it's great. Terrific. Couldn't be better." For some reason Josh was nervous.

Then Randy became flustered. "Oh, I'm sure you're wondering why we're still here. Just finishing up some stuff and you'll have the Manor all to yourself." Then he noticed the valise. "You're not leaving, are you?"

"Oh, no! Ah… listen, in all the craziness, today, I forgot to give you this. I, ah, found it in the bedroom I was dressing in, ah… under the bed when, ah, when I was putting my shoes on. You once said you never went into all the rooms here, and, well, since you're selling the place, maybe you would have never known it was here… there…" Josh was kicking himself for not just giving the damn thing to Randy with no explanation. "Here."

Randy, with Josie behind him, got up and went over to Josh

"I've never seen it before. But thanks, Josh. Now go have a great night and a great life with Katie. We'll be leaving in a couple of minutes."

"Thanks again for such a beautiful day. It couldn't have been more perfect," Josh told them.

Josie gave him a hug. Randy gave him a warm handshake, then a manly hug, too.

When Josh was gone, they both looked at the old, dusty valise.

"Well, open it, Randy!"

With some trepidation, Randy carefully clicked opened the old relic. Inside, there was an envelope, yellowed with age. Randy opened that and read the contents out loud: 'In the event of my early demise and considering the recent financial catastrophe that has occurred in the financial market, this is for my son, Randolph Winthrop The Second, to insure the fact that my legacy will live on.' It was signed Randolph Winthrop The First. November, 1929.

"Yikes! This was written right after the stock market crashed, Josie."

"I know, but what does it mean? A letter in an old suitcase? Was this his idea of a bad joke?"

"Well, from the stories I've heard about the old man, I wouldn't put anything past him. Some legacy. An old suitcase."

Josie looked at that ancient valise and suddenly realized that the letter had been on a fake top. She felt around, found a little tab and pulled it up. They both looked, wide-eyed at the contents in the rest of the case and gasped, screamed, cried and didn't believe what they saw.

There in front of them were bills of money. Many, many, many, many neat stacks of thousand dollars bills.

"Oh my God!" screamed Josie.

"Oh my God!" screamed Randolph Winthrop The Fourth.

Josie grabbed the letter from Randy and read it over. "... to insure my legacy will live on..."

"Oh my God, Josie! This money means I can keep the Manor! I mean, I have to keep it now. Maybe great Grandpa wasn't such a bad fellow, after all," Randy laughed a rather hysterical laugh.

Then he thought a moment, while Josie gently touched the stacks of bills with her finger tips.

"I know," continued Randy. "Maybe I could make the place into a museum or something. You know, a historical monument to my family!"

"Really? I mean, from what you've told me of some of them, especially your father, well..." Josie said with as much tact as she could muster.

"Yeah, you're right. Maybe we could keep having weddings here, or make it into an elegant Bed and Breakfast!" Randy came up with.

"I wonder what else is hiding around here, huh?" wondered an excited Josie.

They sat on the floor, in front of all that money for a long while, just staring at it. Finally Randy decided, first things first. He would pay off all his debts to the bank and see what was left, considering he had absolutely no idea how much was in the valise. Maybe there would be enough to build their own dream house. But one thing was for certain, he would never, ever sell the Winthrop Manor and perhaps one day it would become his sons, then his grandsons, then his great-grandsons.

"You know what, Josie? Maybe all the other Winthrop's failed, but I am going to make my great-grandpa proud!"

"I know you will, Honey. In fact, I think you already have."

And with both their hands still touching the stacks of money, they kissed.

Of course they didn't notice the translucent form of Randolph One, standing near the door watching them and smiling.

Josh was brushing his teeth in the huge, marble master bathroom, wearing only white silk pajama bottoms that Katie had bought him for their wedding night, when Randolph One materialized. Josh almost choked on his toothbrush at seeing him, again. And it was then that the old man told Josh the whole story of what was in the old valise and why it was so important to give it to Randy and the reason he was almost late getting to the wedding.

When Randolph One was in the throes of his own bootlegging days, stiffing gangsters like Benny The Blimp, winning at gambling and making lucrative deals of one sort or another, he kept socking money away for a rainy day and boy did he sock it away. Through the years, he sometimes needed some of it, but then he made more money and replenished the valise. Not even Mildred knew about it. And then, eventually, somewhere in the late 1940's, early 1950's, since at that point things were going well for him and he didn't need it, he just simply forgot about it. Sadly, still not remembering about his stash, when he died he didn't have much in his bank account to leave his beloved Mildred or the rest of his family. Had he not learned that Randy was going to sell his home, he probably would have never remembered. For all those years, all those millions had been sitting in a corner of the attic, unknown of to a living soul.

"Wow," was all Josh could say.

"Thank you so much, Josh. You've saved my marriage and you've saved my home." And then Randolph One disappeared.

When Josh came out of the bathroom, all the ghosts, including the old man were standing by the bed talking to Katie, who was in a white, silk negligee. It was a truly poignant moment, as the ghosts again and again thanked the newlyweds for all they had done for them and Josh and Katie thanking the ghosts for giving them the opportunity to meet them. It was beyond emotional for all of them, because they had a feeling what might well happen soon. And then… sooner than they thought or wanted.

"I have a funny feeling inside," said Mildred.

All the other ghosts agreed, in unison.

"I think something's happening to us. I think, maybe, it's time for us to go," she went on.

"It's been real groovy, guys," said Jimmy, as he twitched, a little.

"I just wish I knew what came next," said a nervous Jack.

"Well, whatever or wherever it is we're going, at least we'll be together. I really believe that, Baby," said Susanna, who then kissed her husband.

"Ya know, I think we just somehow lost sight of how much we really loved each other to begin with. What brought us together in the first place," said Heather, as Jimmy put his arm around her.

And as Katie and Josh listened to them, they saw that the ghosts, now their friends, were beginning to fade in and out of their own reality.

"Now, children, when you two start to argue or fight about things, don't you do what I did. Communicate! Say what's on your mind. I just wish I had done that when I was alive, when it mattered," Mildred said sadly.

"It still matters, Millie. It still matters to me. It's never too late," said Randolph One, as he, too, put his arm around his love and held her tight.

By now, not only were the ghosts fading, fading, but their voices were getting softer, dimmer, as if they were getting further and further away.

"I'm going to miss you, so much..." Katie said in tears.

But before they were gone, completely, Katie and Josh and the ghosts all hugged. But it was so hard to feel them, anymore.

"We'll be watching over you," Mildred said, her voice now hardly audible.

"Maybe you could give us a sign or something, every now and then…"

"We'll try…" whispered Heather.

"We will…" whispered Susanna

And then the six ghosts, the ghosts of Winthrop Manor each took a deep breath and disappeared, first into filmy white forms and then, into… nothing. Forever.

For a few moments Katie and Josh were silent, just staring at the nothingness. There was nothing to see, now and nothing to say. And then…

"Wow," said Josh, softly.

"Wow," repeated Katie.

He put his arm around her and led her back to their wedding bed.

Sometime during the night, when the two were fast asleep, warm and cuddled in each other's arms, a wind blew through the weeping willow tree down below and for no apparent reason, the window slowly opened and the velvet curtains swayed in the night's breeze.

CHAPTER TWENTY-ONE

EPILOGUE

The year was 2010. It was a new decade. But there were still wars that seemed never to end. The ice caps were melting. A lot of bad stuff was going on in the world.

But for Randy and Josie things were good. A few months after Josh and Katie's wedding, they married in a small ceremony at the Manor. Randy paid off everything he owed and had lots left over. When the property down the street from the Manor went on the market he bought it, tore down the existing house and built a new one for his bride, just as his great-grandfather had done.

Josie quit her job at the advertising agency and with love, helped Randy make the Winthrop Manor into a financial success of its own. Every week it was booked for weddings, parties, concerts, political functions. It became *the* place for movie stars to be seen at Oscar and Emmy after-parties and for both local and national politicians to have rallies at. Not that different than the Manor had been at its glorious height in the 1920's. Small conventions were held there. School children visited on field trips to see and enjoy the glorious gardens. And the weeping willow wept no more.

Josie had a baby girl and then another and another. But Randy wanted a son so badly, to carry on the family name that Josie relented and easily got pregnant a fourth time. And finally, finally, one spring day, she brought into the world, Randolph Winthrop The Fifth.

Randy really loosened up through the years, let his hair grow a little longer, started feeling comfortable in jeans and tennis shoes and after getting a political education from his wife, even voted Democratic for the first time in his life. Yes he did! And there was hope.

For Katie and Josh, who kept in touch through the years with Randy and Josie, things were good, also. They had set up their own counseling center which employed a number of therapists. They also gave of their time, helping abused women and old and lonely folks in nursing homes, who had no one to talk to. They visited hospitals to give comfort to the sick and dying.

They had two children, a girl whom they named Heather Susanna and a little boy named Jackson James. At a park, one day, where there was a Pet Adoption going on, they rescued two roly-poly mutts, which they promptly named Millie and Randolph. Yes, through all those years the ghosts of Winthrop Manor never left their hearts.

Where were their friends, Katie and Josh often wondered? Were they alright? Were they together? Had they found some kind of heaven to spend eternity in?

One evening when Katie was in bed, nursing her newborn son, she swore she felt a pressure at the end of her bed, as if someone had sat down there. She even called the ghosts out by name, but no one answered..

Then one day when Heather Susanna was about three years old, she was standing in the kitchen, while Katie was feeding Jackson James in a highchair and the child said, "Who is that lady, mommy?"

"Who, Honey?" Katie asked, the ghosts the last thing on her mind at that moment.

"That old lady, right there, with white hair?"

Suddenly Katie looked at her daughter, then around the kitchen. "Where, Baby? Where is she?"

"She's gone, now. She went away," said Katie's little one.

Every now and again when Katie was alone she was sure she felt a presence around her. It was nothing specific, just a feeling that someone she cared for and who had cared for her, now gone, was there for a brief few seconds. And it comforted her.

And the same had happened to Josh, once when he was hiking the hills, by himself, another time, when he was dozing in his backyard hammock. Just a fleeting feeling that he was not alone. That there was something else. And it comforted him, also.

While alive, the ghosts had had their own pain and frustrations, believing their dreams had not been fulfilled, knowing they had made mistakes in this life. And yet, in death they were able to rectify, at least, some of their behavior when it came to the really important thing in life, that being love.

Where were they now, the ghosts of Winthrop Manor? Were the three couples together in some utopia, in some far away place? Or did they hover near-by, watching, still caring, never really leaving, completely?

Katie hoped so and even the mere thought of that possibility being true made her heart swell.

In death, they had touched the living. Without knowing it, they had left a legacy of love. Or did they know it?

THE END?

The Dark & Light Sides of Fantasy

by R. e. Taylor

Edited by E. a. Waterhouse & Patricia Fry

Published by Shadowlight Publishing
11 Angelina Street, Macgregor,
Queensland, Australia 4109
ISBN# 978-0-9923274-1-5